# The Cuchulainn Chronicles

# The Cuchulainn Chronicles

## Rodger McFarland
## &
## Jonathan White

*Illustrated by Tod Waters*

**VANTAGE PRESS**
New York

This is a work of fiction. Any similarity between the characters appearing herein and any real persons, living or dead, is purely coincidental.

To my wife, Sherra

# Contents

# The Cuchulainn Chronicles

# 1

# The Birth of the Flesh Eater

The moon shone brightly on the thick blanket of snow as three dark figures on horseback crossed the fields with gliding speed. Once again Eagon and his twin sons had crossed the ice bridge into Ulster under orders from King Furbaide of Alba. His orders had not been clear in their minds and he had not given them a reason for their quest.

Eagon and his two sons, Noishu and Rian, rode fearlessly near the land of the Picts. Fifty blue men came out of their huts to challenge these invaders. In their chariots, they gave chase to the mighty warriors, for they allowed no man to pass unchallenged.

The blue men fought naked with their skin stained blue, giving them a terrifying look. Their appearance struck no fear in the hearts of the Alban warriors. They feared only their king and his wrath.

As the blue ones drew near, they began to slow down their chariots. The three warriors stopped their flight and were now turning to face their challengers. Their horses were large and stout, unlike the smaller equines of the blue men. They were covered with matted armor and a bronze head-plate that bore an image of the god of the underworld. Smoke blew out of their huge nostrils, eyes of red glaze stared under the protection of this formidable armor.

Chariots began to come to a halt as the blue men saw

what they had chosen to pursue. Sitting astride the white mount sat a man of gigantic physical structure. Arms hung from a bearskin shirt. They were as large as the limbs of an ancient oak tree. His beard was woven in ropes of hair that fell upon his chest. Long brown locks covered his back as if it had been put there to give him protection. His head was covered with a bronze helmet that came to a peak and a flying eagle could be seen perched on top. He wore the plaid pants of his tribe; the reds, greens, and blacks faded into the deer skin boots. He had the look of a seasoned warrior, indeed the scars were deep and many on his face.

Fear-struck by the look of the massive warrior, the Picts turned their eyes to the other two companions of this giant. Smaller in physical structure, the two younger warriors were nonetheless frightening. Both men were dressed in wolf-skins and identical plaid pants. Their look was that of the great warrior, for they were his twin sons. Long blond hair fell out from the confines of the wolf-heads that sat atop their heavy skulls and their blue grey eyes were that of the wolves themselves. They did not bear the scars of the weathered giant, yet their eyes showed the experience of hard fought battles.

Now turned to confront the Pict savages, battle was a sure thing. Long swords, slid from their casings, shined in the glimmering reflection of the snow and morning sun. Twins they were and when they fought together, no man could defeat them. With stabbing spears and swords in hand, they looked to their father for the command to charge. He knew his sons were ready to draw blood on this day, but his years told him that he needed to give the blue men one more scare. Slowly, he reached in the bag that hung on the side of his war-horse. The great axe slowly appeared and even slower he raised it over his

bronze helmet. With a mighty Celtic war cry, he charged the enemy. He then waved to the young ones to attack.

"Dispatch these blue children with haste, we have a mission to perform," he yelled. Following close behind his father, the first son gave a terrifying scream. "Let the lesson begin, my father." Soon, the second son was beside his brother. They drove their horses into a group of Pict chariots. As they passed, the heads of two drivers rolled helplessly on the ground with their eyes blinking at the deadly surprise. At the same time, the old warrior gave a mighty swing with his axe as three blue warriors charged at him. Blood spewed from a severed arm, half a skull hit the ground, and the guts of the third fell into his own hands.

It was enough. The blue Picts, who were more farmers than warriors, had been beat up by every tribe on the island. It did not take them long to see the might of these invaders from across the frozen waters. Besides, they had done their best and could go back to the village with only a few dead—against such a worthy foe. This was as good as a win.

Having expended only a small effort, the three warriors were ready to continue their task at hand. "Father, can we stop long enough to clean our weapons?" asked Rian. "We have a long journey ahead, we must not waste any time. If we do not return to the ice-bridge before the half-moon, we will be stranded here. "How much farther must we go?" inquired Noishu.

"Tomorrow we will reach the fields of the deadly winds. We will cross them at night as not to awaken the wind goddess. On the far side of the easternmost field, we will find the magic oak tree. There we will find the nature of our mission," said their father. The urgency of their quest prevented them from hanging the heads of blue ones on their mounts as was the practice of their tribe.

The fields of Ulster were a fearsome sight. Flat and wind blown, they laid silent before the warriors. Nature was the ruler of the minds of the pagans and nature ruled their lives. Their gods were all connected to nature. Those who dared to challenge the gods soon found out who controlled the elements of their world. This night Nantosuelta, goddess of the winds, slept, the winds were calm and the moon was bright. The end of the quest was near. The warriors sensed success and flew like eagles across the fields.

"The tree, the tree," cried Rian. In the darkness, the tree's shadow shone; cast in the lustful light of moonbeams. The riders slowed their pace and stopped at the foot of a grand oak tree. Quietly, they moved forward. Then, they stopped at the foot of the oak. "Father, what do we do now?"asked Noishu.

"Wait." In a short time, we will know our mission," his father responded.

At the same time in a nearby peasant hut, a stout blonde girl was groaning in the pains of labor. Attended only by her younger sister, she screamed as the first birth pains started. "Oh sister, please find someone to help me."

"There is no one who will help in this birth. They all believe that there is something very unnatural about it," the nurse responded. Coughing from the smoke that filled the hut she sat up in the hay bed, her eyes bulging with tears and shouted, "Teutates, I will sacrifice this child in your name, for I want it not. This child of rape is unpure, the smell of death was on the monster king that did this to me. I will not raise anything from the loins of an evil flesh-eater such as Furbaide."

5

As the three warriors approached the sacred oak, a voice rang out. "Who comes to the tree of Sucellus?"

"It is I, Eagon, sent by King Furbaide Fer Benn, ruler of the dark provinces."

"Yes, I know him well, the one that smells of death."

"Tread lightly who ever you may be, for I am sworn to defend his honor to the death."

"Honor? Honor you say? Is it honorable to eat the heart of the former king of Ulster?"

"Worse things have been done. Besides, he did so to take his powers of the long vision." The winds picked up and snow began to blow hard at the three warriors. "You have aroused Nantosuelta, she does not like your arrogance."

"It is best that you tell her to stop her games, or I will rape her as my king did the daughter of Conchobor King of Ulster."

The winds slowed as fear began to overtake the wind goddess. The winds died and the young sons of Eagon lowered their skin robes to look upon Sucellus, who had come down from the tree. His appearance was that of the very oak in which he lived—fingers of small branches, legs of the roots and mouth and eyes which were nothing more than knots. "Let me have a look at the man who does not fear the gods."

Thin and gaunt, Sucellus presented little threat as he approached Eagon, yet still the sons drew their swords. A small wave from their father and they lowered their weapons. Sucellus raised his palm to the face of the warrior giant and a glowing light appeared in his hand. "I know you. You stood next to Furbaide when he feasted on our good King's heart."

"It is so, and as I remember you decided to put your lot with us on that day."

"A god sometimes has a hard time looking after his own interest. As you are aware, Conchobor had plans to cut down my trees to create more pastures for his great bull. The magic of the oak must never be lost by human disrespect, so I stood with your king."

"Enough of your dribble. Our king has sent us to you to find out why you summoned him and what was the purpose of the message about a birth that is to take place." Eagon was a man of action and he knew his time was getting short. Sucellus's slow manner was unnerving to the warrior, but gods of the forest and agriculture were known to take their own good time.

"There is a manchild to be born tonight in Ulster. He bears the mark of the flesh-eater. You must find this child soon before harm comes to him. I have paid my debt to Furbaide. Now it is up to you to find the child." Eagon roars, "This then is our quest?"

"Yes," said the god.

"We will find this child tonight and return him to our king," shouted Eagon.

"That way will lead you to your prize." Sucellus pointed to a light in the distance. Three men mounted and rode with much urgency. As they rode off, the tree god returned to his place in the sacred oak. He watched from afar and said softly, "Best for the world if they are too late. This will be no ordinary child."

The closer the riders got to the light, they noticed that it was a large fire that made the yellow glow. Two figures stood next to the consuming flames. In the hands of the smaller figure lay the outline of a newborn. Sensing danger for the child, Noishu pulled his bow and strung an arrow. With the skill of many battles in his aim, he let the arrow fly at the small female form.

Cethe stood before the sacrificial fire she had built to

do honor to Teutates, god of the tribe. Finnada, daughter of Conchobor and the mother of this newborn, stood by. She was weak from the unholy birth, but she wanted to see this child devoured by the consuming fire. As her sister raised the child above her head, Finnada saw a flash shoot from the flames. Cethe stood frozen in death as the arrow lodged in her throat. Slowly, she lowered the child to the frozen ground. The warm red blood ran from her mouth and baptized this male child.

In shock, Finnada stared at the flames, wondering why the god of her tribe had refused her gift. Then, as if the gates of the hell had opened, three dark warriors rode through the flames and dismounted. Rian rushed to the child that lay comfortably warm in Cethe's blood. All was well as he wrapped the infant in a sheepskin. Strangely, the child did not cry, he only stared deep into blue-grey depths of Rian's eyes. A cold shiver ran through this warrior that had never experienced fear before.

Eagon approached the exhausted mother. "Finnada, you should be honored, you have given birth to a future great king."

"I have laid the egg of death and pestilence and I curse my womb for carrying this messenger of woe."

"I command you to feed this child so that we may be on our way," Eagon roared.

Finnada, sensing that she had control of the situation, began to laugh in a challenging manner. "Oh, so it's my milk you wish to use to nourish this death angel?"

"Feed this royal child, it bears your blood as well as our king Furbaide's."

"Never let it be said that my breast suckled this monster child."

"My lady, you leave me with no choice."

Turning to his sons, he motioned for them to hold

9

Finnada. Eagon picked the child from Rian and moved toward the princess.

In a cold damp castle in the land of eternal darkness, the flickering candle burned low. In this dim light, Furbaide closed his eyes and smiled at the scene that appeared before him. The long vision worked well, although Conchobar had been a little too greasy, but he was a meal well spent. The king was proud of his choice of warriors for this task. The child was of little importance, but Furbaide had only two daughters and a manchild would be a better candidate for the king at his death. As he closed his eyes once again, he smiled at the sight that was taking place before him.

Eagon moved to Finnada as she struggled to get away from the twins. Celtic and strong, she battled with her captors, but the birth had taken her strength. There was a time when she fought by her father's side. Many heads hung from her saddle and time and again she had broken ranks and led her father's troops to victory. Today, it was the young bulls of Eagon that would win the battle. Eagon pulled at her wool gown. It fell, revealing the muscular body of this Celtic queen. Her legs were dark from the dried blood that ran from her as she bore the demon. Her breasts were full of rich milk that was meant to feed her newborn. Eagon pushed the child to the round breast and forces the nipple in his mouth. Finnada cursed Eagon. "You will live to regret this day. There will be much pain for you Eagon. I ask Cernunnos, the horned one, to put a curse on you and your sons." As she spoke, the child bit the nipple of her breast. Surprised by the event Eagon pulled back. He looked into the eyes of the child. What he saw was a chilling apparition and he forced himself to dismiss what he saw. The blood ran from the small mouth that was full of pointed teeth. Finnada laughed, seeing fear in the face of the fearless warrior. Eagon in full rage, screamed, "Bitch, it is you that will suffer my curse." Raising his dagger he cut into her breast. "If you do not wish to feed your own child, then I will become the midwife." He then placed his wine pouch under her breast until the milk and blood mix filled it. "This prince will nurse on your milk, even though you turn him away." The child was content with the feeding of milk and blood. Rian placed him in a fur-lined bag on the side of his horse; they traveled on to Alba to the fort of Furbaide. Finnada lay dying from the wounds Eagon had inflicted on her. She watched as the warriors rode out across the cold, snow-covered fields. Weakly, she said but one word, *Cuchulainn.*

# 2
# The Hound of Ulster

Nantosuelta; goddess of wind, streams, valleys and all things to do with nature, had been deeply offended by the invaders from the dark land known as Alba. She had feared a mere mortal and this hurt her gentle manner. As she listened the night of Finnada's brutal death, she sent a breeze on the wings of a raven to take her last word to the one to which the name belonged . . . Cuchulainn.

The raven was the messenger bird of the goddess Danu. It swooped down and took the word in a breath then flew to Sliab Cuilinn, the mountain where The Hound Of Ulster had been long recovering from his mighty battle with his friend and equal in warfare, Ferdia Mac Damain. Much had happened in the absence of the defender of Ulster, the worst had been the invasion of the dark warriors from across the icebridge. Cuchulainn had laid helpless with wounds that would have killed a normal man. Almost a year later, he had regained his strength and skills, which he had traded at birth for a chance to live a long life.

While practicing atop the mountain the skills of sword, bowmanship and the deadly stabbing spear, he saw the sign of the nature goddess—the raven. He wondered if there was a purpose for this visit. He was close to several gods who protected Ulster and her hound. He knew that gods would help a human as long as he or she

13

was willing to the terms of the gods. Sometimes the terms were harsh, as in his case.

Suddenly, the raven settled to the ground in front of Cuchulainn. He watched as the raven slowly began to change its shape. A bright light blinded The Hound and he was unable to tell what was happening. As his sight returned, before him stood a figure of such beauty that he could not speak. She had the face of a goddess, but she was wearing a long black robe that was covered with the feathers of the raven. It was Danu—the earth mother.

Cuchulainn smiled. He had been on the mountaintop way too long. He needed a woman in the worst way. Could this be the answer to his dreams and prayers? Not just a woman, but a goddess of awesome beauty. Her lips were the color of rubies and her eyes shone blue as the waters on the high mountain lakes. This was all he could see, but it was enough. His heart began to beat with expectation.

Then, she spoke, "I know what you want and I am sorry to disappoint you, but I am just a messenger for Nantosuelta."

"If that is all you are, then you are correct, I am disappointed."

"I came to tell you of the grave events that have taken place in this past year. As you lay at this place licking your wounds, much misery has fallen on the kingdom of Conchobor. The nation of Ulster was overrun by the savage warriors of the king from across the waters. They came for only one reason: to gain the power of the long vision." Cuchulainn no longer lusted.

"This power of the long vision was the gift of the gods to my king."

"Yes that is true, the king of Alba now owns the power."

"There is only one way a mortal can take the power."

"Yes, that was the way it was obtained." Heart broken because of the news that the great king who had been like a father to him was dead, and, even worse, was consumed to get the vision, he began to cry. Danu spoke again,"There is more bad news."

"Please tell me everything."

She told of the rape of Finnada and of the two sisters' deaths after the birth of her child. Few knew that The Hound had much sisterly love for Finnada and Cethe. Upon hearing of their horrid deaths The Hound screamed and the trees bent to the sound. He pounded the ground so hard that all the rabbits and small creatures ran from their burrows.

Danu was surprised to see the warrior show so much passion. She felt his pain. As he knelt, she put her hand on his arm. He looked up to see that the goddess had removed her robe. She took him by the hand and led him to his hut.

After they had entered, they moved to his meager bed and sat down. He was a mighty warrior but there were no luxuries in his arrangements with the gods. A warrior must live a hard life to stay strong for battle. The goddess did not look to the surroundings for her interests were with The Hound and not what he owned. He was young, seventeen, and a lustful sight to any woman. Long rasberry-blond locks tumbled to his shoulders from under the leather headband, thick lips with a rose color and his massive body that had drawn many women to his bed.

Cuchulainn was still struck with the news of what had been his only family. Knowing his thoughts and his pain, Danu started to desire this man of deep feelings. "I knew that earlier you desired me. Is your pain such that your man need has gone away?"

He raised his eyes to once again gaze at the magnificent sight. Now there was more to see; the robe that had covered her body was gone and the gauze garment that she wore revealed all that he had forgotten about women. His loins began to ache.

His hand was rough as it moved up the soft leg of this creature. She was unlike the warrior women that had filled his needs in his short life. Her face was smooth, free of the roughness so common in human females. A tear ran slowly from the eye of the great warrior and as it reached his cheek, he felt her warm lips kiss it from his face. Her breath was that of honey mixed with rose petals.

*Could this really be happening, or was it a dream produced by the fever that had come and gone in this last year?* He reached for the small waist that was now so near to him and encircled it with his huge arms. She was drawn into the hair-covered chest that thrusted outward each time his heart beat. Slowly, her soft lips touched those of Cuchulainn. This time, it was a kiss of passion and not sympathy. As he slipped between her milk white legs, he was sure he was not having a dream.

Bright sunlight burst between the oxhide that served as a door. The Hound slowly began to awake. His senses were slow and somewhat confused. Suddenly, he thought of the goddess and begins to search for her. *No, wait, surely it was a dream.* Although his body told that his man needs were relieved, he could not consume the thought that he had really been with a deity. As he sat up in his rock-hard bed, he saw the proof from the messenger. A raven feather, black and shiny, lay in the place of the beauty that had laid there the night before.

The Hound knew that his life was to be short and full of challenges. Small pleasures were to be taken lightly, but this had been a little different. He now was dealing with a new task. The warrior must avenge the crimes that had been dealt Ulster in his absence. Sword, shield, spear, war chariot, armor and the gifts from the gods were his tools of his trade. He gathered all of these together. The time had come for The Hound of Ulster to once again protect those in his need.

# 3
# Gathering of the Tribe

The Land in the Sky was the name given to the isles of Ireland and England by the early Celts. When the great ice had gone away, a large channel of water had formed a barrier between the mainland and what now looked like a piece of land floating in the sky. The early Celts had arrived by sea and by the sky. Cuchulainn was the descendant of Celts who had come by sea and spent their time cleansing the isle of the first inhabitants, the Picts. This was the practice of the nomadic tribes of Europe.

The legendary people that had come from the sky had become the religious leaders of their time. They were called the Tuatha De'Danann. Their goddess was Danu.

As The Hound traveled past the streams near Cualinge, his memory raced, for this was the land that he had stood against the entire army of Connacht. King Ailill and his queen, Medb started the whole thing—it was the result of their own desires to try and out do each other as far as their personal possessions. It came down to who had the greatest bull. Medb could not present a bull to challenge the fine bull owned by King Ailill. In her search for such an animal, the word came about a fine bull owned by the King of Ulster. She made him an offer to buy this animal, but he refused. Being a warrior queen, she decided to come to Ulster and take the prize possession. A strange sickness took charge of all the Ulster men.

So, there was only one to stand the challenge, Cuchulainn.

His thoughts were not about the many warriors he had dispatched in this war, but of only one, Ferdia mac Damain. Cuchulainn's friend, Fergus mac Roich, was a man of Ulster who had fought bravely in the defense of Conchobor and had been king at one point. As a child warrior, Cuchulainn had looked on Fergus as a true friend. They fought side-by-side on many occasions, covering one another's back. Fergus was not as good in the king's court as he was on the battlefield, and this proved to be his downfall. He fell from the king's favor and joined the ranks of the Connacht cattle raiders. On this day, The Hound was set to fight Ferdia, Fergus' foster brother. Fergus came to Cuchulainn and tricked him into not using his special battle techniques.

Mighty warrior against mighty warrior, it finally had to happen. All the warriors sent against The Hound had done him little harm. Each had tried different methods to defeat the mystical one, but none could defeat him. It was Ferdia that stepped forward at Fergus mac Roich's call for someone to face the challenge of The Hound. The stream ran red with the blood of these combatants. Hunks of flesh flew from the fallen. Their cries of battle frightened anything alive in Ulster that day. The fury of Ferdia was paramount. No warrior could stand against him. Cuchulainn did all that he could do. He called upon his salmon leap only to remember his promise and then took still another stroke from the blade of Ferdia. On this day, The Hound was forced to run. His wounds were massive; no man could have fought with more valor. He could not call upon his warp spasm because he had to honor his agreement with Fergus. It was truly the day of Fergus mac Roich and his foster brother, Ferdia. The next day, in

a terrible state, Cuchulainn faced Ferdia again. Ferdia saw the weakness from the previous day's wounds and felt that this day The Hound would fall. Not to be, for today the weapons of the gods were in place. The warp spasm and finally the *gae bolga* finished the young warrior Ferdia. Cuchulainn was sad in this victory for Ferdia had been his friend, but it did not stop him from dispatching a multitude of the remaining army of queen Medb. Thousands died that day. Kings died alongside common warriors; women and children were not spared. The carnage was enough to weaken the forces of Connacht, and when the men of Ulster recovered from the illness—they ran Ailill and Medb's armies out of Ulster.

Scars from that battle still reveal the test that the young warrior had withstood. He was still alive to defend his motherland, Ulster. He wondered how Fergus mac Roich had faired since their last meeting. Cuchulainn had no hate for him, only respect. He realized that if he had not been so battleweary, he could have dispatched Fergus as well, not something he wished to do.

Emain Macha, the center of life in Ulster, was in total disorder. Since the death of Conchobar, and now the murder of his heirs, no one wished to take command. Life had become a cheap commodity. Food had become the only thing of value. Daily, people lost their lives for an apple or a hunk of pork.

As he neared the gates of the once beautiful city, The Hound saw poverty and beggars. Human filth was strewn on each side of the road. No one recognized him as he rode through the squalor. At the gate, a drunken soldier with a whore on his arm looked to make an attempt at a challenge. All his drunken eyes saw was a large warrior and he made no attempt to stop The Hound's progress.

In the middle of the courtyard stood what used to be

the common house, where the king would came to meet with his people. Cuchulainn dismounted his horse and entered. To his surprise, the commons was now a brewery house.

At one of the tables sat a man that Cuchulainn recognized. "Mac Roth," roared The Hound.

The man leaped up from the table drawing his sword, "Who would challenge Mac Roth this fine day,"

"Shall I challenge an old friend to fight?"

Mac Roth stood blind, but the voice was one that he new well. "Thank the gods The Hound of Ulster is alive."

"Of course I am alive, you old battle ax. Are you so drunk that you cannot see me?"

"Alas, great warrior, I am indeed blind, thanks to the dark invaders from Alba."

"So not only do they eat our kings, they also blind our best warriors," quipped The Hound.

The alehouse had been covered in silence since the name of The Hound had been spoken. The word had been that he was with the gods in the underworld. *Was he really back or just another joke from the gods that had deserted them?*

A young beggar boy stood in the corner. Dirty and sick, he eased forward slowly. Quietly, he moved up behind The Hound and touched his leg. With lightning speed, a dagger was at the boy's throat. It had been drawn with such speed that no one saw it being pulled from his belt. The boy did not flinch, he was too sick to be afraid of death. The mighty warrior knelt, and looked the boy in his eyes, "You know that I am flesh. Only you had the courage to test me." The silence broke into cheers of relief. Truly, The Hound of Ulster lived and had come home.

Cuchulainn mac Sauldaim placed his arm on the young beggar's shoulder and led him to the table where

Mac Roth had taken a seat. "Mac Roth, what has happened to the people of Emain Macha?"

"Fear, young lord. They fear the return of the dark ones."

"The men of Ulster have never known fear of any enemy. What have these dark ones done to draw such cowardice from once great warriors?"

"They are not cowards, they have no one to lead them."

"Yes I know," he said with regret in his voice.

Seeing the great warrior drop his head in shame, the young boy spoke, "It was not your fault. Everyone knows of the wounds you received in the defense of Ulster."

"Thank you for the support, but I was sworn to defend our land under any circumstance. It was my place to die before running from any enemy and especially Ferdia." Lifting a horn of ale, Mac Roth took a long drink and wiped his mouth clean with the sleeve of his cloak. "On any day but that day, Ferdia could have never been your match. You had fought and sent hundreds of warriors to their graves. Your wounds were massive before you took on that young warrior." Feeling the face of The Hound, Mac Roth bellowed, "Your scars bear witness to the punishment you took for Ulster and the proud men that lay sick with the strange illness." Looking up to Cuchulainn, the boy proudly said, "You were our hero then and you can be our hero now, please take control of Ulster and lead us in the revenge of our King Conchobor."

In front of a large fireplace at the castle in Alba, stood Furbaide. He was surrounded by many guards dressed in skins of animals they had killed in recent hunts. These were the best of the dark warriors. They did not love their king but they stayed his loyal servants out of fear. The smell of death was something they had long grown used to. Chained to the wall were prisoners of their latest raids in the eastern part of Alba. Furbaide bore the look of the early Celt warriors, his hair was a faded red, long to his waist, braids were full of jewels taken on his visits from the purses of his captives. Gold earrings swung almost to his shoulders, a breastplate was his constant companion. Many a blade had dented this plate in attempts to rid Alba of his plague. Those who lived through these attempts soon learned why this king of darkness was so feared. Mercy was a word that had never crossed his lips. His pleasure was the pain of others. He had been matched with a queen of equal desire. She was a master at the worst thoughts a human could congeal. Nothing was more delightful than the total pain of others.

Tonight was a special night. The quest of Eagon was bringing them a new toy. Heavy footsteps sounded in the hallway, a sound that the king recognized as Eagon and his sons. But on this night, there was another sound strange to the castle, small steps. The guards swung open the doors to reveal the three giant warlords followed by a toddling child. They approached their king, giving no support to the child. Magda, the queen, stood at the side of her king. Their teenage daughters, Trell and Wanda, sat on pillows nearby. The loyal warriors had been true to their task. They knelt to the king and queen. Furbaide leaned forward to get a closer look at the child wrapped in wool.

"What are you trying to do to me? I sent you to bring me a man-child of my blood to put in my stable. I ask for a pony, you bring me a warhorse."

Eagon replied, "Great king, we have brought to you what you have asked for."

"Fool, you have been on the return from Ulster for three days. You expect me to believe that this is the child

I saw in the long vision?" A fearsome fit of rage took over the king. "I'll have three heads on pikes before midnight if you cannot explain this boy."

"Lord Furbaide, we slept briefly on the second evening. In our usual manner, two slept while one watched the darkness. The child was placed near the fire to keep him warm."

Eagon was beginning to sweat as his empty stomach growled for relief from the stomach acid that gushed. Suddenly, he began to vomit nothing but bile.

"Why can't I get someone to explain what has happened here," screeched the king.

Magda stepped forward, "Perhaps our brave warriors have lost their desire to please the king."

Noishu replied, "Do not blame my father for his inability to speak, it's the curse."

Noishu stepped up to the queen's feet and began, "As my father began, we were resting just this side of the bridge of ice. The child was quiet and all seemed normal. I slept, and my brother slept as well. Eagon would not sleep for fear that something might happen to the child. Our father was tired and drifted in sleep as fog began to fill the campsite. Suddenly, a sound like no sound any of us had heard before raised us all to our feet. We thought it to be the sound of the war horns so we each grabbed our weapons. Then, through the fog we saw Cernunnos—the horned one. The sight of him made us all fall to our knees. Then, he moved to the child and lifted him to his chest. Eagon ran forward but the fog confused him and he had to return to the camp. As we waited for the fog to lift we heard the sound of an animal eating. We looked to the sound and suddenly we saw what looked like the child but older and larger. He was eating something. As he drew close, it was then we saw that he was gnawing on the skull of a human. He had part of the brain in one hand, then we saw the head that had the face of Rian. My father has had this illness since this sight."

"This story smells of failure and a poor attempt to cover up a misdeed."

Rian spoke out, "If you doubt us, simply speak to the child."

"You expect this toddler to respond to speech? Ridiculous!"

"Only try, sir, and you will find the answer."

"Alright, boy can you speak?" The small boy came into the light of the candles, the daughters covered their eyes, and the queen moved behind the king as he leaned forward in delight. "Speak, boy."

He spoke,"I'll take no commands from you or anyone else. I will speak when I desire." The king looked into the body of a child, but the face and eyes of an animal. His teeth were sharp and pointed, skin covered with fur, ears that looked like that of a boar hog and eyes red glowing as if filled with blood. The worst of him was the smell of flesh on his breath.

The king was happy with his newfound son. He bent to ask the evil one a question. "Do you hunger?"

"Yes," he said. Laughing, the king pointed to one of the prisoners chained to the wall and yelled.

"Then feed yourself."

The child of horror ran to the struggling man and tore an ear from his head, then consumed it. The king and queen looked to each other, as the queen said, "I think he will fit into the family just fine."

Back in Emain Macha, Cuchulainn had taken shelter in the hut of Cuan mac Roth. He had barely noticed the small figure that sat quietly outside the door. The first day of the return of The Hound had been discerning to him. A once proud people had turned into a rabble of thieves and drunkards. This angered him, although he felt as if he had deserted them at a terrible time.

Outside, the young boy rolled in half-sleep and knocked over a stool. Mac Roth turned to the warrior, "Did you hear that?" Cuchulainn had his great sword in hand and slowly pulled the cowhide door cover. He eased through with caution but with no fear. He hoped for confrontation to once again test his warrior skills. This would not be the night for a test as he moved to the boy sleeping on the ground next to the hut. "Boy, wake up." His voice was like the sound of thunder on a mountaintop. Quickly, he jumped to his feet. With a large stick in hand, he charged the giant figure. "Woe, boy I am not your enemy." Awakening, the boy realized that he was attacking the one he admired. "Forgive me great one." Smiling, Cuchulainn honored the boy, "Your courage is that of the true men of Ulster. Tonight you will be my back." He took the stick from his hand and placed his own dagger in its place. "Come in and sleep near the fire. Help yourself to the stew my friend Mac Roth has made for us. Tomorrow, you will start learning what it means to be Cuchulainn's back." The glistening eyes of the ten-year-old stared from beneath matted hair and dirt. He could not believe what he was hearing. The gods had favored him this day.

The next morning, the three unlikely companions walked across the frost covered earth toward the wooden stronghold. This had been the home for the king, queen, and their warrior daughters. Now, it was home to about two hundred dark warriors that had been left by Furbaide to rob all they could from the people of Ulster. As the word passed through the city that The Hound had returned, frightened hearts grew strong with courage. Old warriors began to dig up swords that were buried over a year ago. Great axes appeared from barns, hidden in cow manure . . . wives began to sharpen spear points that had been used as cooking tools. As in the past, the women of Ulster were ready to stand with their men to rid the once proud land of the common foe.

As the three walked through the streets, warriors began to fall into ranks behind them, for on this day a leader had returned and he would never allow the foreign ones to have comfort while the people of Ulster suffered.

A fearsome sight, Cuchulainn was in full battle dress. His long reddish-blonde hair could be seen under his bronze helmet. He carried his axe over his right shoulder, in his left hand was a stabbing spear with a four inch round shaft. His breastplate gave praise to the gods that had given him his warrior skills. A new god had been skillfully carved into the plate—it was Danu. He had a large shield strapped to his back. His face was handsome even though it showed the perils of accepting the warrior way. The aging Mac Roth carried only a long spear with a large shaft. Even though he was blind, his other senses had taken over. He had dispatched many a warrior with his skillful use of the stabbing spear this last year. Smell and hearing were his best aids. The boy had come to cover the back of The Hound. He had but the dagger given to him and a sharp pointed spear he had made from a branch. It was not the weapons of this boy but his courage that gave him a warrior's way. Cuchulainn looked at the boy who was a small reflection of himself. At the age of ten, The Hound had fought in hundreds of battles and slept with many women. It was difficult for him to realize that he was only seven years older than this boy.

By the time the three had reached the fortress, they were joined by a hundred men and women warriors looking to do battle that day. Guards at the fort had closed the gates and their calls had brought out the entire garrison. The leader of these troops was Budack Boak. He had been left by King Furbaide not to rule but to maintain fear as his control factor. Of this he was well-qualified and had been constantly leading raids that included senseless killings, rapes, and the theft of all the food he could obtain. He enjoyed the site of burning bodies but did not have his king's taste for human flesh. Nevertheless, he met the high standard of evil that his king demanded.

Budack stood on the wall of the wooden fort and looked down at a ragged bunch of dirty men and women. He turned to his second-in-command, "Casey, why have you called me out from my meal to see this disgusting gathering of Ulster trash? Do away with them then come to my quarters."

"But sire, there is now a leader."

"So, bring me the head of this rebel. Now, on with your task."

In desperation he yelled out, "But sire, it is The Hound; Cuchulainn."

He was stunned to hear the name. "Cuchulainn, I was told he had died from wounds inflicted on him."

"Even so, there is a large warrior wishing to talk with you."

Budack leaned over the wall and looked down. His eyes met those of The Hound and he knew immediately that the warrior still lived. "What do we owe the pleasure of this visit of the long absent defender of Ulster?" Angered by this statement, Cuchulainn responded by spitting on the ground. He then looked up to Budack, "Be gone from Ulster before this spit dries."

"Ha, ha, so The Hound has a sense of humor."

"The Hound has no sense of humor when it comes to the dispersing of shit like you. The spit drys as we speak,

30

soon you will watch your own entrails burn. I understand you enjoy seeing Ulster men burn, maybe you will enjoy watching Alba men burn as well."

Not liking what he had heard, he turned to his archers and waved a signal for them to fire on the crowd. Arrows flew from the wall, many Ulster men fell to the ground and some turned to run. Cuchulainn, seeing the fear take his warriors called out, "Hold and follow me." Covering the boy and Mac Roth with his shield, he ran to the gate. As he neared the gate, he called upon himself to do the salmon flip. With mystical strength, he jumped and his body turned into the salmon. All on both sides were struck in amazement as he cleared the top of the gate. When he touched the ground, he returned to his earthform and killed two guards with one blow of his mighty fist. He then pulled the gates open and the men and women of Ulster charged through.

A mighty Celtic battle began. The men of Alba fought bravely this day, as was their way. Spears pierced bodies and blood ran as water in an Irish trout stream. The people of Ulster found their lost courage and revenge tasted sweet. Their leader fought as a madman, heads fell like wheat in the spring. The boy not only covered the back of his master, but cut a path through the opposing warriors so that The Hound could reach the warrior Budack.

Budack was no match for Cuchulainn and he knew so. In less than thirty minutes he had seen his two hundred warriors be cut to pieces by ax, sword and spear. The body parts of his men lay strewn in front of him. When all this came to be, he decided to try and escape through a little known exit behind the barn. He mounted his horse without saddle or reins, being a great horseman this would not hinder his escape. He looked back to The Hound waving his sword. *Augh,* thought Budack, *I am free from the threats of this bragger.* As he left the exit, a large blonde woman warrior unhorsed him with a stick. Several Ulster men grabbed him and carried him back into the fort.

The battle had ended when the Alba warriors had seen their leader run for his life. They threw their weapons to the ground in the midst of the bloodsoaked battlefield. The sight was common to these people that lived daily with death. Bodies were in all places, some dead, some dying, and some wounded badly. These were times that revenge was honored, this left little hope for the captured and wounded warriors. Those townspeople that had not joined in the battle now served their purpose. They began to strip the clothing, weapons, and anything of value from the dead of both sides. They killed the wounded Alba warriors and helped the warriors of Ulster. The captured warriors had no chance of surviving unless they could bring money from the slave traders.

Cuchulainn's day had gone well. Most of all, he had once again led the mighty warriors of Ulster. This would be a start of the army it would take for him to avenge the death of Conchobor, his queen and the daughters he had loved. This was not indeed a good day for the warrior Budack. The Ulster men carried him to the feet of The Hound. "I warned you to leave, but you did not take me seriously." Looking at his captor, "Do as you will with me, but you will face the wrath of my king Furbaide."

"Who should fear who, scum?"

"Your king left you here at the mercy of what ever might happen. He is no one to admire or fear." Sensing death was near, it was the nature of the Celtic people to die proud. "So you wish to kill me by burning. I say let it begin."

In most cases, Celtic people would have honored the

braveness of this warrior but he had left a trail of blood, rape, and burning that could not be ignored. Cuchulainn pointed to a rock altar, that was used for sacrifice. The warriors dragged Budack to the rock, then they tied his hands behind his back. The Hound motioned for them to tear the wool shirt from his body. His pale white chest was laid bare, then they stripped the rest of his clothing from his body. "Anyone whom this man has wronged come forward and take your revenge." Many people walked out to have a last chance to give the captive a small sample of the pain he had so quickly administered. Some cut small slices into his body others spit or urinated on him. Cow dung and human dung was smeared on him.

After all had their opportunity, it was time for the worst of the ritual. The Druid priest came forward to perform a sacrifice as to appease the gods that had helped the Ulster men on this day. A lamp of hog fat was brought forward by a Druid priestess. Once again, Cuchulainn motioned to the warriors to lift their captive up to the altar. The priest said a short prayer to the gods. He raised a large knife over his head and blessed its purpose. He then began, with surgeon-like care, to cut across the stomach of Budack. The blood that ran from the wound was collected by the priestess in a large bowl. The captive winced in pain, and sweat burst on his forehead. The pain was much worse than he expected. All present hoped to hear him scream for mercy as their family members had at their burnings and rapes. The entrails were slow to fall from the open wound, so they were pulled forward and placed over the hog fat flame. Trying hard not to scream, Budack bit his own tongue in half. Finally he could stand no more, he let loose a Celtic warcry in defiance, then died from the shock. His body was then cut to pieces so that his afterlife powers were not bound together.

As this scene took place, Furbaide watched with the long vision. He cared not about his loyal warrior, but was focused on the threat from The Hound of Ulster. It was good that the icebridge had melted and made it very difficult to enter his kingdom. Also, he needed time for his own warrior to grow. This was happening at a rapid pace, thanks to the curse and a steady diet of enemy flesh.

The people of Emain Macha were happy in their victory and the revenge they had felt this day. Ale flowed and the streets were full of people dancing and eating from the fortress food. All seemed good since the guardian Hound had come home.

All had gone well for the three warriors today. Mac Roth had been a worthwhile part of the victory and the ale was good on his lips as the celebration reached its peak. The boy had fought as a man and fought well. But that did not mean near as much as the friendship and love he now felt for mac Roth and for Cuchulainn. As for Cuchulainn, he had fought harder battles and had been praised before. He knew that he must perform two more tasks. One was to raise a large army to help bring the long vision back to a rightful successor, and the other was to see the goddess Danu one more time.

# 4

# Finding the Lost Warriors

Cuchulainn, now driven by revenge, set out to find the brave leaders that once led the men of Ulster. He took along the boy and Mac Roth. Mac Roth had stayed in Emain Mancha mainly because the dark ones did not see a blind man as a threat. Little did they know, he was the main source of information to all the banished warriors. His clever guise had given him access to the heart of the encampment. His hearing was that of the fox and the smelling ability of a hound. All this came to his aid as a source of information to what was left of the Ulster army.

The three headed southeast to Irard Cuillenn. As the men of Ulster were defeated by the invasion of the Alba hoards, they drifted to Irard, which bordered Connacht. They were free to enter Connacht only if they would swear loyalty to Fergus mac Roich, and his queen, Medb. Some entered his ranks but most turned to face certain death in battle with the invaders.

Trapped between both forces, Finian mac Odhran, the only leader left, called on Fergus to meet with him. Finian, knowing the lust for women that lived in the heart of Fergus, had both his beautiful daughters at the meeting. Large amounts of beef were cooked along with trout and all the vegetables that were left in their camp. Why not use the last sources of food? Soon, they would be dead or slaves.

Fergus arrived at sunset. He was accompanied by all his close relatives, the only men he could trust. His appearance was that of a much softer man than his warrior-history should allow. The fact that he had been a king allowed him a very dignified look. One might say he was arrogant in his manner, but this had proven in his favor with the women. He had been spending much time in the bedroom of Ailill's queen. His stately manner had taken Medb, but also Fergus was hung like the breeding bulls of Connacht.

As Fergus entered the hut of Finian, he was taken by the two young girls. "Welcome to our meager hut," announced the Ulster leader.

"A good day to you old friend, you have raised two fine hefers."

"My thanks Fergus, for you are truly a great judge of womankind." The young girls, even though they were warriors, served the meat, fish, and vegetables to these men of Connacht.

"It is important that we discuss my reasons for calling you out on a night so bold," mashed Finian. What he was about to do was not his way. He loved his daughters, but now was not a time to hold back any tactics that might save the men of Ulster. Morrigan, the older of the two came forward to pour ale into a drinking horn. As she moved closer she allowed her breast to be seen by Fergus. His eyes sparkled as he glared at the snow-white mounds of pleasure. Ale ran down his chin and disappeared into the mass of hair that was his beard. "Why is it that you have summoned me here this day?" he asked.

Finian took a large drink of ale to boost his courage. "You are aware that we have no place to go, nor can we defeat the dark ones. If I must beg, than let the begging begin." Fergus took a bite from the roasted beef then yelled loudly that all in the camp could hear, "There would be no begging for you and your men if you had only joined ranks with me." In a soft voice as not to challenge Fergus, Finian said, "We are men of Ulster and you of all people should know that there are those of us who would rather die than side with Ailill and Medb." Lowering his voice, Fergus eased closer to this brave man. "Finian, you speak well, but why am I here?"

"Help us. We need you to send the word to the ones from Alba that you stand with us and they will not attack."

"And if I do this for you old friend, what can I expect in return?" Sickened by his own words, Finian spoke out, "You can have my daughters for your own pleasure till the solstice moon returns."

Looking at the second daughter, Bridget, he saw even greener pastures to plow. She had not fully developed and had the sweet smell of youth. Blonde and strong, yet not unlike a piece of fresh fruit. He looked to Morrigan, "Have you been with a man as yet?" Boldly she spoke, "Yes, he was a warrior of Ulster that had the courage to stand against a hundred dark ones. He was a true Ulster man who would have never left his nation and fought against her."

Having been called a traitor before, he was not upset. Indeed, he liked the fire that this shining star shone. "Deal. I will send word to the men of Alba to be gone, or face the mighty sword of Fergus mac Roich." With this, he gathered up the daughters of Finian. Turning to Morrigan, he asked, "What of the warrior that soiled you?" As she mounted her horse, she replied. "He killed the dark ones until his sword broke and his spear shaft snapped, and then he died for mother Ulster."

"A brave but foolish young man, now I will have to

show you what a real warrior's weapon is like. I assure you that my shaft will not break."

He did as he said he would do. The dark ones retreated back to Emain Macha and finally to the icebridge that led to Alba. Finian and the men of Ulster were told to stay where they were by both the dark ones and by Fergus. They settled as best they could and became farmers. Finian died soon after this event from a broken heart, for his love ran deep for his daughters.

Due to the death of Finian, there was a struggle among the Ulster men to find a true leader. Unexpectedly the second wife of Finian stepped forward and claimed the right of leadership. Gwydion stood the challenges of ten warriors who decided a woman was not worthy to lead them. All ten came in the night to dispose of her leadership and her life. They did not know that the goddess Sheela-na-gig had given her the night-vision and a stabbing spear that was invisible. The next morning, ten heads adorned the horse that she rode among the other Ulster men. All were asked to challenge or follow. She had earned her leadership. She decided that the land they were now prisoners in would be called Meath.

It was a fair ride for the three warriors from Emain Macha to Meath, but the gods were happy with the return of Cuchuliann. The sun took the chill from the air and the site of the fields, streams and mountains gave strength to the spirits of the travelers. As they rode closer to Meath, Cuchuliann thought that he had never asked the boy his name. "Boy," shouted The Hound. "Tell us your name."

"Why does it matter about a name as long as I cover your back?"

Not used to people talking to him in such a manner, Cuchulainn knocked the boy from his mount. "When The Hound asks you a question, you just answer, goddamit."

"My name is my own and I have the right to keep the name to myself and if you knock me from my horse again I will be forced to fight you." Mac Roth sensing something in the boy's reluctance, said, "Here, here, we must not fight amongst ourselves, we have only three to bring back the army of Ulster." Cuchalainn boasted loudly, "This boy of no name must learn that I am the one that took him from the streets of Emain and gave him food and weapons to defend himself. He must tell me his name, if he has one." "I was good enough to cover your back, when I had no name, why is it of importance now?"

"I tire of calling you boy."

"And I tire of calling you Cuchulainn; The Hound. What is your real name?" The warrior spirits of both began to boil, then Cuchulainn said, "Setanta mac Sualdaim."

"What?" grunted the boy.

"Yes, my real name is such. I was called The Hound after I killed the great and much loved Hound of Ulster. As a boy, I acted the role of a guard dog and the name stuck to me."

"I too will reveal my name to you and Mac Roth, but you must let no one know who I really am," said the boy. Laughing at the arrogance, both warriors swore that the boy's name would never be revealed by them. "I am Adian mac Marlon."

"Mac Marlon, the son of the most powerful man of magic in the land in the sky." Cuchulainn stepped down from his horse, and with a booming laugh, lifted the boy from the ground. "Not only are you brave, you have the best imagination of anyone I have yet to meet." Adian muttered in the ancient language, *"Loch domd-a-dae hoc aug neu bane laville."* Suddenly, The Hound was lifted in the air and thrown over the saddle on his steed. Landing with a thud, the huge warrior lost the breath in his lungs. The air that blew from him toward the sea, which was many miles away, spun the gentle fisherman's boats around and around in the green sea of ancient Ireland. Quickly recovering, he took a hard look at the boy of small stature. There was a new respect for he knew that magic was the strongest of weapons a warrior could possess.

The word had passed that The Hound was on his way to Meath. Gwydion dressed herself in the warrior armor of the times in case Cuchulainn was after taking charge of her army. Her beauty was only in her strength and her ability to lead men and women into battle. She had formed a legion of women warriors that fought as a unit. These women warriors had raided into Leinster and returned with cattle and farm animals which had sustained the men of Ulster during the hard times. This group of women warriors were especially frightening during their monthly time of purification.

When they finally arrived, they were witness to a grand site. The entire army of Ulster lined the road and shouted praises for The Hound. In the celtic tradition, Cuchulainn began to sing of his great prowess. He began, "Yes, The Hound has returned to defend Ulster. As in the past, I will clean our soil of all invaders, I will slaughter as many as they can send to confront me, for I am The Hound of Ulster and until now no warrior can boast of the triumphs that I have achieved in my seventeen years." He jumped from his horse and the dreaded warp spasm began. His eyes bugged out on the stems and fell upon his cheeks. His skin drew up to the top of his head and then reversed its position on his body. The calves of his legs turned backwards, then from his thighs came great spikes. The lungs shot from his mouth and settled on his chest as the skull began to swell and the sinews in the back of his neck grew as large as that of a bull in heat. The rut was on with The Hound and only three things could return him to his normal self. The first was simple—to fight and slaughter thousands of descendants and bathe in the blood of his prey. The other was to have sex with as many women or men as he could before the sun has set. The last was the most common reaction and that was for him to be washed in ice-cold water three times. Needless to say, this method was the most preferred by the men of Ulster.

Before the warriors came with the ice-water, a hundred Ulster men died of fright at witnessing the terrible warp spasm. It was as if death itself had appeared this day on the plains of Meath. When the horrible sight was finished, Gwydion rode out to greet the visitors and showed herself well by challenging Cuchulainn to battle. "The Hound of Ulster has proven his greatness by the gifts bestowed on him by the gods. I stand here with the help of only one goddess and she is of the lower realm. Let us test each other's power in one on one battle, then we will decide who will command the men of Ulster."

"I did not come to take your command away from you, but instead I wish to have you and your men stand with me as equals, even though you are not." Gwydion stepped forward and with all her warrior manner, she said, "I know the strength of The Hound and all of Ulster needs this power to regain the lands that have been ours for five thousand years. I will stand with you as your equal even though I know The Hound can never have an equal. But first you must allow me to test your manhood in my bed."

That night, a great feast was held in honor of the return of Cuchulainn. Large sides of beef were roasted and brought into the hut of Gwydion. She saw fit that The

Hound was given the first cut of the beef, as was the ancient way. Ale flowed as if there would never be another cask of ale brewed on this emerald isle. "Cuchulainn, why did you desert us for so long?" asked Gwydion. "The wounds from the war with Connacht were deep and withering on my body. I fell into a deep sleep and spent months in the presence of several gods. They spent their time healing arms, legs and deep injuries in the chest and belly. You can judge me as you will, I live only because the gods wish me to live."

Gwydion moved closer to The Hound and laid her hand on his thigh, "I know that you were and are now The Hound of Ulster. I will follow you wherever you wish me to go." The Hound had consumed his share of ale, and his staff was becoming alert to the occasion. Adain moved to the warrior and respectfully said, "One of honor, please let us go now." The Hound turned in drunkenness, grabbed the boy by his head pulled him into his face, "This warrior woman has need of my special gifts on this night."

"Dear sir, you are into the ale, for surely you could not be willing to have love with one so ugly."

Pulling the young man forward once again, he said "Perhaps you are just jealous that I can have her and you cannot."

"Believe me sir, if you so desire, you must do what you must do."

"Well then, boy of magic, make her beautiful for me." In complete disgust, he looked to the lady warrior, she had moved very close to The Hound—so close that the hair under her arms lay upon his shoulder. The young one looked upon her body and gagged for she had no form at all. The smell of dirt and rotting food in her teeth was enough to disgust any sober man. The ale had done its

43

harm to Cuchulainn . . . also he had not had sex since the dream of Danu. His member was at full attention and his wits were blurred. Once again, the young one said, "Are you sure you want me to use my magic to fool you into believing you're with a beauty, rather than a horse face?"

"My needs run deep and I must unload my manhood into something, be woman or man."

Fearing that The Hound, under the influence of the ale, may turn upon his own youth and lust after him, Adain once again called upon the ancient language, *"Cosh acaw lom tang tu tatu."* The Hound turned to see the warrior queen as the form of Danu. He drank the rest of his ale then fell upon Gwydion with extreme passion. This alarming sight cleared the hut. As the young one walked out with Mac Roth on his arm, he said, "Tomorrow he will probably kill me."

"Only if he does not kill his own self, for sure The Hound longs in desperation for the companionship of a woman of any nature—YUCK!!!!!"

The next morning, Cuchulainn returned to the hut that the three warriors were given for their stay. He moved slowly, for his head felt as if it had grown to four times its size. His eyes glowed red as the sunset and his secret weapon was sore and abused. "Good morning my friend,"said Mac Roth, who had heard him leave the abode of Gwydion.

"Damn, you old blind fart, why must you yell at the top of your voice?" Chiming in, Adain, in a much louder and annoying tone called out, "Oh, the mighty Hound seems more like a pup this fine morning."

"You had best fix me something to put on my stomach." Standing up, the blind one approached The Hound with a horn of stale ale, and held it in front of his face. "Away, you devil of a man."

"I see that you walk with some discomfort," sang out the boy. Cuchulainn wrenched with pain, "How did I end up with a woman that looks like a man when I went to bed with a goddess?"

Adain laughed out loud, "The ale was stronger magic than my own. I could only put the image you wished for in your mind, the rest was up to the ale."

"The worst is over, for now she will join us in our revenge and quest for the long vision. I would like for both of you to know that I nearly took my own life when I woke up to find my nose buried in her hair. It took all my courage to open my eyes. Fortunately, it was her armpit, not something to be proud of, but better than the other." They all burst into loud laughter.

# 5
# What of Fergus?

The Hound not only gave of himself, but he had promised Gwydion that he would return her daughters before the march to Alba. This would mean a face-to-face meeting with Fergus. The Hound had missed the presence of this great warrior, yet he did not know his mood since he had killed Ferdia. Matters not, there were a large number of Ulster warriors in his ranks that may want to return to their home nation.

It was but a day's ride to the capital of Connacht, Mag Cruachan, and they had only one obstacle and that would be the Sinann River. Gwydion had put herself alongside the odd threesome and this made their strength greater for she carried the invisible spear and sight in the darkest of nights. The four possessed many gifts from the gods and these gifts would be needed in the months to come.

As they approached the river they dismounted their horses and led them to the water's edge. Suddenly, in the middle of the water, there began a great disturbance. Streams of blue green water shot high into the air, forming a rain cloud from which came streaks of lightning and rolls of thunder. The wind blew so hard that it drove water into the cheeks of the warriors and made it impossible for them to see to their front. The horses bellowed with fear as a large face appeared in the middle of the storm cloud. It had bushy eyebrows with a large bulbus nose that ran out to great rolling jaws. The eyes were dark but had an air of mischief and the voice was rough as if the voice was made of thunder. "Who dares to water their mounts without the permission of Tristan?"

Mac Roth cried out, "Please forgive us, oh Lord of Disorder, we only desired to relieve the thirst of our horses and of ourselves."

The face opened its mouth and a lightning bolt shot to a nearby tree setting it on fire followed by a huge clap of thunder that sounded a lot like laughter.

Cuchulainn picked up on the laughter and began to realize that this was a minor god having fun with mere mortals. This was not uncommon since pagan gods were living with humans each day in some form of nature. Contact was constant with minor gods and they became friends or enemies as was the occasion. If you had a flood, then that god was not in favor with you on this day, if the sun shone brightly and your crops grew, then you and that god were in favor . . . very simple.

On this day, the minor god of disorder was simply having a little fun. His mistake was to have fun at the expense of The Hound. "Damn you, Tristan, do you know who I am?"

Tristan grumbled, "I know that you are a presumptuous human that failed to pay tribute to the great god of riot and disorder."

"Why would I, The Hound of Ulster, pay tribute to such an insignificant god that can only make little storms that disturb our progress only briefly?" Upset by this human insult, Tristan decided to play his hold card. Answering The Hound's challenge, "So you're the child warrior that laid sick and allowed your nation to be overrun by warriors, whose god is that of the underworld."

Cuchulainn responded, "Be careful, minor god of little power, or I will take what small pride you obtain away from you." Angered, Tristan called out the guardian of the river.

This was it, the best he had to challenge this mere mortal. In the ancient word, that not even Aidan knew, he began the call, *"Irrus temair kolb fletch kon dar, losch teremall tum kalm toomed da harraer."* Turning to Aidan, Cuchulainn asked, "What the hell did he just say?"

"Shit, I don't have any idea."

"What of you Mac Roth, what did he say?"

"I heard a druid priest use the very same words thirty years ago. I don't know what the words mean, but I remember the results and I am getting my ass out of here right now." Grabbing the reins of his horse, he attempted to mount, but it was too late.

Bubbles began to come from the river. As they popped in the air, they released the smell of sulphur. Gagging on the smell and unable to move, the four warriors stood frozen at the sight arising before them. Out of the depths of the river Sinann rose a disgusting sight. It was a scaly hunk of undescribable form. A mass of swamp weeds covered the fishlike head and two large flapping arms stood out from the body like fins. There was a long tail that swung back and forth and on the end it boosted two sharp pointed horns. It had a long jaw that protruded from the face, its smell was awful. When it moved, it left a trail of something similar to snake dung.

"You had to go and piss off a minor god," complained Gwydion.

"Oh shut up, it's no big problem. You can just bitch it to death," said Cuchulainn. Mac Roth came forward and grabbed Cuchulainn's arm, "Please do something quick, the smell is about to burn my nostrils out."

The Hound looked to Adian, "Well, dammit, do some magic and make it go away."

"Can't do. My magic only works on humans."

"Augh shit, I guess I'll have to rid us of this minor road block myself."

As the huge slug dragged itself on to the bank, Cuchuliann drew out the mighty axe. Yelling at the top of his lungs, and then holding his breath, he did his salmon leap toward the head of the monster. Just at the right time, the monster opened its mouth and swallowed The Hound of Ulster. Cuchulainn's companions stood in shock, the great warrior had been consumed by a monster conjured up by a minor god.

Looking down from the cloud, Tristan began to laugh, "So much for the mighty Hound of Ulster. I suppose I am not such a minor god after all." Suddenly, there was a great splashing sound as the stomach of the monster burst open. Standing inside was The Hound with his axe in hand. He had opened the pet of Tristan and took away the only form of defense that the minor god had. Reeking of guts and blood, Cuchulainn stepped out and drew his first breath in several minutes. He looked up into the cloud, "That's the end of any power you may have had, minor god. Now you will see that anything we request is done rapidly."

He then moved to his friends, who immediately retreated from the smell.

"Goddamit, I almost gave my life, and now you will have nothing to do with me?"

"Please great warrior, just a little dip in the river and me thinks all will return to normal," said Mac Roth as he held back his desire to puke.

"Yes, a wash couldn't hurt,"said Gwydion. The Hound thought that indeed he must smell bad if Gwydion

would have nothing to do with him. At last he looked to Adian. Holding his nose, he pointed to the river. Not used to bathing, Cuchulainn went to the river with reluctance.

He looked up with disgust and said to Tristan, "This is worse than your guardian. I will expect a favor in the future." The face in the cloud smiled and said, "Okay."

Clean and shining like a new gold coin, The Hound led his party to the gates of Cruachan. This was the royal town and many merchants, traders, farmers, warriors, and of course, whores filled the streets daily. This town received merchants from as far away as Greece and Persia. They brought the luxuries of the day. Gold jewelry was the most desired by the Celts, along with fine fabrics and silk. The traders of Connacht were famous for their most desired products—slaves. The town had prospered while the land of Ulster had gone backwards. They could have taken Ulster at any time but there was nothing there to desire. The king had settled his bed talk argument with Mebh and he had gone about his business of building a great trade center out of Mag Cruachan. The queen was happy for she had a prolific lover in the warrior from Ulster, Fergus mac Roich. Had not the king been so busy this could have been a real interesting situation. Mac Roich was bold enough about it all, and he set up a place to stay near his lover's fort.

The city was far ahead of its time due to so many outside influences, but still held with the celtic architectural design. A long, well-built road had been built with the help of the Etruscans who sailed to the small harbor at Irrus Domnann. There were thousands of residents and the surrounding countryside was full of farms worked mostly by slaves. This food was another trade item that kept the warring factions on the continent well-fed. All was good and the chances of invasion were unlikely for no one wished to see the prosperity end. Wooden walls with ramparts surrounded the city. Even though they were lightly guarded, the watch was constant. On the outside of the wall was a ditch with no purpose. It had filled with water and was used by the poorer subjects as a water supply. Inside the wall, a city of huts were laid out in good order. Ditches had been dug to take waste and run off water out to the moat. Wells had been dug deep into the earth to make sure that in time of siege the townspeople had a water supply. The huts had small corrals and a barn. Animals were kept inside in winter and were sent to surrounding fields to graze in the warm months. Ducks were popular, but not just for food. They, as well as the chickens, were family pets and eaten when they grew old. Beef and game were the main source of food. They had developed a system that worked well for the longterm storage of food. Holes were dug in the ground and lined with several layers of rock and pebbles. Covered with wood and hay, the food stayed at a safe temperature. The lower part of the town was at the bottom of a mound, the lesser residents dwelt at the bottom and the king and queen at the very top.

The sun was rising when the four strangers approached the gate. A challenge was called out, "Who comes to Cruachan?"

"We are traders from Leinster come to speak with mac Roich about the purchase of slaves."

"Do you come in peace? For if not, you will surely die here."

"We come in peace," said The Hound.

The small gate in the main gate opened. It was just large enough to allow the horsemen to dismount and lead their steeds into the booming city. The sight was almost too much for the men and woman from Ulster.

The smell of food was in the air. Vendors were already on the streets selling food and drink. Merchants were setting up their wares for the day's sales and slaves were being awakened so that they might be moved to the auction areas. Whores were bathing in large barrels of water that was heated enough to keep them from freezing up their working parts. As the four warriors walked by, in amazement, a whore called to Adian, "You, young one. Come over here so mama can take a look at the big dagger you carry."

Several other ladies of the night came to her side in the window. They began to call to the boy, "You are so pretty, I'll bet you belong to that rugged looking man."

In anger, Adian yelled back, "you call me a pretty boy? Well none of you can hold what is in this pretty boy's pants."

"Boy, you brag well, I hope you can back up your claim," said the blind one. "My claim is that none of the whores will take what I have in my pants and I bet the only gold coin I own."

"You have a bet, bold warrior, but if I win you must use your coin to buy me the best looking whore in the hut."

Cuchuliann interrupted, "Old fart, what difference does it make if she looks good? You're blind!"

"Well, you may be right—okay boy, I want the best-smelling one."

"I am among the sickest of men. We are here to get my daughters back and all you can think of is whores," ranted Gwydion.

"Don't worry, this will not take long. If the boy can make his boast and if he loses, the old man will be finished in five minutes. Now go get yourself some breakfast and we will come over shortly," says Cuchulainn.

Adian walked slowly toward the laughing whores. By this time, there is crowd gathering to see how the boy would fair with his boasting. As he neared the window, more whores came to taunt him. One called out in a loud voice, "Are you a stallion or a gelding? We will soon find out, ha, ha, ha."

Another joined into the action, "I am so afraid of the size of this infant that I am sure I will faint when I see it."

Nearing the window, he reached for the tie that held his loose plaid pants up. The Hound and Mac Roth were standing just behind his back. They were far enough away not to hear him quietly say the words. *"Ach na cone walhgh nare loga."*

"Tell me what you see the boy doing," asked Roth. "I cannot see around him, but he is lowering his pants now."

Screams came from all the whores and most turned to run back into the hut. The whore that said she might faint, did faint, the townspeople ran away as if they had seen the evil god Allobrox. The young one called out to the disappearing whores, "Doesn't anyone of you want what's in my pants?"

"I guess not. I want to know what happened," questioned the old man.

Cuchulainn responded, "I am not sure. All I saw was the whores running away from the boy's pants."

"Old one, your bet is lost and you owe me a gold coin, ha, now I have two gold coins."

"Boy I must know, are you so endowed as to frighten off professional women?"

"Old one, all I said was will any one of you take what was in my pants and none would."

Cuchulainn stepped up to the old man, "Don't let this child have his coin until we are sure he won."

"No, it's a fair bet, I will give the boy his coin."

Adian looks to the eyes of The Hound, "You think I have cheated, or maybe you are afraid of what's in my pants."

Laughing, Cuchulainn said, "I don't fear the gods so what makes you think I would fear your small sausage?"

"Okay, then, here it is." The boy dropped his pants and the head of a huge snake lunged at The Hound. He let out a loud yell and then started to roll on the ground in laughter. "What can be so funny about a young boy's penis," said the old one, shaking his head.

"Alright you have all had your fun. Now how do we find my daughters?" asked Gwydion as she finished an oat bread muffin.

"Finding Fergus should not be a problem. He will be in or near the queen's quarters," commented Mac Roth. "When I was the messenger in Emain Macha, there was plenty of conversation about the sexual activities of Fergus and queen Mebh."

"I think it best that we ask someone the way," tuned in Adian.

"That's a great idea, but did you think that someone may recognize me?

"You know I did kill several thousand of their brethren," barked The Hound.

Mac Roth spoke up, "We have come as men from Lensiter, looking for slaves and I am sure that Fergus will receive us. I am not sure how he may react when he is confronted by The Hound."

"We will worry about that when the time comes, now we must locate him," said Cuchulainn.

As the foursome headed deeper into the town, they could see the quarters of the king and queen. All the streets were going uphill for the town was built on a mound. At the midway point, there was a second wall but

this one was made of stone. It was there to give more comfort to the royal family and to make an invasion more difficult. This wall had iron gates and was guarded by the special troops who were assigned to do nothing but protect the king and queen. Behind this wall, life was somewhat different than that in the streets below.

A second group of people lived in extreme luxury. Even though the townspeople lived well at a time of economic boom, there was a huge spread in lifestyles. Those who were lucky enough to live behind the rock wall were a select few that were directly associated with the king or queen. In the quarters of Fergus, life prospered as well. He had the queen's favor and of course, free access to her quarters. His abode was not quite as lush as some others, but it was large enough to house his chieftains and top ranking officers. He also had room enough for several young ladies that he referred to as his nieces. Among these nieces were the daughters of Finian and Gwydion. They had lived well the last few months. Fergus was a man of gentle nature when it came to dealing with women, but his appetite for sex was too great for him to allow them to go untasted. He spent most of his time with Morrigan, who swore a curse on him each time he took her. The truth was that she had appetites similar to that of a warrior, for she bore the name of a warrior goddess. She would battle Fergus in the bed to the point that they were both covered in sweat and bite marks. For the warrior Fergus, it was not unlike the many times he had been involved with the taking of women during raids of his youth. For Morrigan, it was her show of independence and total resistance to a man taking her without her willingness. In reality, they both enjoyed the struggle. Fergus feared that someday he might be forced to really do battle with her when the solstice time arrived. As for

Bridget, he had simply kept her around to sing songs of battles past in Ulster and to tell stories of the little people. He did so love these stories, and also her young age had slowed his assault. There was another reason . . . his son Gavyn had expressed his love for her.

Fergus was having some ale and bread with some of his generals when a guard entered the room, "Sir, you have slave buyers from Leinster at the gate, they wish to have audience with you only. This is a bold bunch."

"Tell them to go to the auction square like all the rest."

"But sir, they said that they wish to buy all the men slaves from Ulster."

"What?"

"These are indeed bold Leinster men, send them to me."

The guard turned and hurried to the gate where the four were waiting. "Fergus will see you now, but you must disarm before entering the fort." Cuchulainn was first to hand over his sword and spear. Next, mac Roth gave up his spear with staff. The boy handed over his selfmade spear. The guards laughed, "This is a weapon to fear, is it not?" sneared the head guard. "How many heads has this thing of beauty put on your saddle?" cried out another guard. At this point, Adian was about to lose control. When Cuchulainn laughing with the guards said, "But of course, didn't you see them, but maybe rabbits heads are too small to see?" They all laughed loudly as the young boy entered with his dagger still in his belt. "And what of you warrior queen, shall we search you for weapons since you do not seem to carry any?"

"Please, help yourself, but be sure to search me well," she said while she smiled almost toothlessly at the guards.

"Ugh okay, one of you search her," suggested the main guard.

"Hell no," echoed the youngest guard. "I ain't touching her, it's up to you," snarled the older guard.

"Alright, alright, I'll do it. Lift up your cloak." As Gwydion raised her arms up to hold the cloak open, her body let out an odor that would cause the mightiest bull in Connacht to run through a rock wall.

"Stop, please, we can see that you are not armed, go ahead." So now Gwydion had entered with the invisible spear.

The guard led them through the upper mound streets. Houses were much larger. There was just one large corral near the gate across from the guards quarters. It was well-stocked with cattle, hogs, chickens, goats, and a lot of sheep. The meal of the day was taken up to the main fort located at the extreme top of the mound. There it was slaughtered and sent quickly to the kitchen area. All the king and queen's associates ate well at least once a day. After that, they had to fend for themselves. Most shopped in the village below.

The women they saw were well-washed and most wore a lot of gold objects on their person. Their dress was mostly wool but woven into designs. Some wore the plaid of their family tribe, while others wore tributes to their favorite god. Most of these women were wives and daughters of chieftains and high-ranking officers. Others were slave gifts from traders wishing favors from the people that ran this mercantile settlement. The rest of the people living there were the financial supporters, warriors of high respect, and druids who were the religious connection. This area smelled much better than the streets below. All of the waste from this island of plenty was sent below as if it was a gift to those less worthy.

The guard led the travelers to a large hut near the top of the mound close to the stone fort that housed the king. They were taken by several sleeping rooms and an inside wash area. Some of Fergus' lovely nieces were in the middle of their baths. In a low voice, Mac Roth spoke to Adian, "Is that what I think I smell?"

"What do you smell, old one?" said the boy.

"I smell the sweet flesh of young women, fresh-washed in rose water."

"It is as you say."

"It is in these occasions that I miss my sight the most."

Cuchulainn had his head covered with a hood, while Gwydion, who looked like a man, wore a bronze helmet of a Leinster warrior she had killed on a raid. They were taken into a large room where fifty warriors stood. Dressed in a breastplate and half-armor, just in case this was an attempt on his life, Fergus sat on a stone chair covered by two bear skins. He always looked as if he were still king of some nation. "Come forward slowly, please, so that I might see the slave buyers wishing to buy all the Ulster men. You see, I cannot sell you slaves from Ulster, for all that dwell here are warriors that decided to come into my ranks by choice. I do have slaves for sale if that is your true intent."

The impressive figure of The Hound came around the large open fire that warmed the hut. Keeping his hood over his head, he looked into the faces of many Ulster men he had fought with against the very people they now dwelled among. "Good sir, you have found us out. We in truth have not come to buy slaves. In fact, I have come to ask you to let these brave men return to their homeland."

"This voice . . . this voice is one that is familiar to me, yet it cannot be, for The Hound of Ulster lives no more."

"Wrong, dear Fergus, not only do I live, but I have come to free the slaves that you call your warriors." As The Hound dropped his cloak to the earth floor, a loud sigh of fear came from all the warriors and Fergus.

"Have you then come to kill me bold warrior? For if you have it will not be an easy task." asked Fergus.

"You need not fear my intent, Fergus mac Roich. I have come to take back those warriors that wish to fight again for Ulster." As the two men stood at the face off, Gwydion stepped forward, "So that there may be no mistakes, we have come to get my two daughters as well."

"Who is this man that would talk to me in this manner?"

"Man, you bastard, I am the wife of Finian and the girls that you hold in restraint are my daughters." As Gwydion stepped forward into a fighting stance, Cuchulainn grabbed her and pushed her back to Adian who held her by both arms. "I have come too far to meet with Fergus and I will not allow a woman to disturb what I have to say." The warriors in the room had all drawn their weapons, but only in the defense of mac Roich. An old friend of The Hound came forward from the ranks, "Cuchulainn, have you returned to lead us once again in battle against our enemies?"

"Indeed, I have come back from the grave for no other purpose," said The Hound.

The warrior looked to his mates and says, "He is back, thanks to the gods." Then to the surprise of Fergus and The Hound, they all yelled out the ancient warcry of Ulster, "*Sliab Fuait.*" They broke ranks and surrounded The Hound with great affection. Hugs and kisses were exchanged. All stood with Cuchulainn, for the chance to be led by The Hound was a great honor. War was the way of life for true men of Ulster and they had been too long in the good and easy life. Some had lost their spirit, but not their love for Ulster. Their chests were suddenly full of pride and the real feeling of manhood crept into their loins. The Hound was alive, and The Hound was back to raise the courage to the level that made the men of Ulster the great warriors that had sent the Irishmen back to Connacht in defeat and shame. Fergus moved slowly toward Cuchlainn; his tears were building in the corners of his eyes, for he was a true man of Ulster. He looked deeply into the eyes of The Hound and said, "Brother in battle, I have missed you. Even though you have killed my foster brother, Ferdia mac Damain, it was a fair fight that almost ended your life and I tricked you so that your special tactics could not be used. I missed your strength and fearlessness in battle, for no warrior can be your equal."

The Hound moved to Fergus, putting his arm around his neck,"How could you leave us to be among these people of Connacht?"

"I was decrowned and forced to honor Conchobor as king. I could not accept this disgrace, so I elected to regain my position by leading the forces of Queen Medb in the *Tain Bo Cuailnge*."

"The truth is that I did not lay one sword's edge to any Ulster man, I remained in the rear ranks as an advisor."

"What is your position now that there is no heir to the throne?" asked The Hound.

"Indeed there is an heir of royal blood, and that is my son Gavyn."

"It is true that he is of the line, and is deserving of the throne; In fact, he is still loyal to Ulster," cited Cuchulainn. At this point, a young warrior stepped around Fergus. He was taller than The Hound by several inches. His blue eyes shone with his youth, and his body was marked with battle scars. He was not yet carrying the belly of the ale drinkers, nor did his face show the wear and tear of the cold winds that ruled the island. He was as if cut from stone and his muscles were hard. His arms were somewhat longer than normal and provided him the gift of throwing a spear for a great distance. In fact, at one point in battle, he had taken out a proud king that felt as if he were at a safe distance to enjoy the sight of the fight. His voice was deep even though he was only fifteen years old. The makings of a beard was on the tip of his chin. His manner was indeed kingly and his stride was that of a man of pride and honor.

"I have seen you in the defense of Ulster, mighty warrior, and I know your love of our land. I, too, did not take one life in the cattle raid, but do not let yourself think I did so in fear. I, too, love Ulster, and I wish to return and take back the land as well as the god's gift of the long vision," announced Gavyn, in a princely manner. "I have come to take all who would face a horrible foe from across the dark waters. You will not be handed the kingdom. You must prove that you are worthy by bathing in the blood of the men of Alba." Gavyn took the mighty hand of The Hound and said, "It is my good fortune to finally fight beside The Hound of Ulster, I will go with you." All the warriors raised their voices to the man and once again rang out the warcry,"*Sliab Fuait.*"

Unknown to the warriors, the guard, who was a man of Connacht, had left the hut and was on his way to the quarters of King Aillil. He had seen their most dreaded foe in the heart of their city and was off to give the alarm.

Back at the hut, a decision had been made that all Ulster men were to march out with The Hound, but there was still Fergus and the daughters of Gwydion. "Forgive me for my mistake in assuming you were a man dear

Gwydion, and I am sorry about the death of the good Finian."

"There is no problem in mistaking me for a man for I am any man's equal in war or in bed. The time is up for my daughters to return and I am here to see if your abuse has harmed them in any way. If so, you will die this day."

"Brave warrior, you will see for yourself that the fruit of your womb is in good stead. But also know I have done as I pleased with them for that was the agreement. Indeed, if you request battle, I have no fear of a mere woman."

"I'll show you the revenge of a mere woman if my daughters have been treated poorly," raged the woman warrior.

Fergus sent for the girls and then turned to The Hound, "I would that I could go with you back to Ulster, but I cannot, for in truth I have made a promise to the Queen Mebh. I will stay here in her court by choice. The truth is that I love her more than any I laid with before or after."

"Father, I have stayed with you since my mother's death, and now I hear you say that you love the queen more than you did my mother."

"T'is so my son. As fair as your mother was, a man must love and lust in time of her absence. I have found it hard to love only one woman at a time, but my love for Mebh will keep me in place."

"Father, you make our parting much easier."

"Let it be so my son."

The daughters entered the large room, having been freshly washed, they were a sight to behold. They ran to their mother and all began to cry. In spite of the fact they were warriors, they still had the feelings that are more common with women than men. "Has this man harmed you in any way?"

Morrigan was first to speak, "He did only what was expected, and beyond that he treated us well."

"T'is true mother, and of me, all he ask was to hear many stories of the little people."

"Fergus, I thank you for your kind ways," said Gwydion. "These were women of Ulster, I only did of them what they deserved," responded Fergus.

Gavyn looked The Hound in the eye, "How are we supposed to leave this fort without being seen, or do we fight our way out?"

"Well," resounded The Hound. "I really had a good plan to get us in, but I never thought about getting out. I guess we must fight."

"Wait, maybe I can help. We can wait until dark, then I will lead us out the same way we came in by the scent we left," said Mac Roth.

"Great idea," chimed The Hound. "Let's move to the door and see what we will have to face tonight." As the men of Ulster walked to the door, Fergus left to go to the queen's quarters.

Slowly, The Hound pulled open the woven cloth that covered the entrance to reveal five hundred guards and Connacht warriors. "Oh shit," cried Adian. "What do we do now?"

"Fight," resounded The Hound.

"Well there is still another way," said Mac Roth, "I can still lead us through them, if our young friend can come up with some smoke."

"Well, you can put snakes in your pants, now let's see something worthwhile," said Gwydion.

"Okay, okay. Just give me a little time to conjure up a spell."

Cuchulainn, looking out the door, said, "You had better hurry. They are beginning to move in on us."

"*Koch lett nach borne dade boriax decom dot,*" spouted Adian. All at the door looked out hoping to see the magic bring forth a covering smoke, but nothing was happening. "What's going on here?" asked Gavyn.

"It's the boy, he knows magic," answered mac Roth. "Well, I just started a few months ago and it's hard to get all the words right some time."

"Goddamn, boy, are you saying you can't make the smoke?" asked The Hound.

"Sure I can make smoke, if I got the words correct."

"Well, it looks like we are going to have to do it my way." All the warriors started to draw their weapons. "Wait, It's not *decom dot,* it's *dacom deet.*"

"For the sake of the gods, say it right," cried Gwydion. Quickly, Adian repeated the chant with the right words. The Hound had already broken from the hut and cut two guards into halves. Out came Gwydion, with no apparent weapons, as the second wave of guards ran at her. She began to strike out with the spear that could not be seen. Warriors and guards began to fall, screaming in pain. Those behind them stopped the charge and stood in silence, stunned by the death of their fellows. Blood flowed as King Aillil watched from his window. It was once again the menace of The Hound that was making him look unworthy. This time he would finish this pain in the ass himself once and for all. He took the golden bow from its place on the wall and returned to the window just in time to see The Hound draw his axe and began to wade through a mass of Connacht men. Arms, legs, and large pieces of flesh began to fly throughout the courtyard. A true killing machine was in action and only a golden arrow could stop him. Ailill strung the arrow and started to let fly when the guard standing next to him screamed as a spear ripped into his chest. It had been intended for the king and his loyal guard stepped into the path. Looking for the one who had thrown this deadly spear, the king spotted the son of Fergus who saw that the king would do harm to The Hound. Once again, he aimed the arrow at The Hound and drew but he could not see him for a cloud of smoke had covered the battle scene. His anger was so that he almost passed out. The son of the queen's lover had almost killed him.

The smoke filled the courtyard and the battle stopped for no one could see their enemy. Mac Roth came walking through the smoke sniffing and calling out to the Ulster men, "*Sliab Fuait, Sliab Fuait!*" They all began to join hands and began their journey out of the city. As they went through the lower streets, the old warrior continued to call out the war cry and hundreds of Ulster men came from their huts to start their trip home. It was but a short trip to Meath and Cuchulainn gathered the troops of Ulster to go home to Emain Macha.

As for Fergus mac Roich, he was taken from the bed of the queen just at the point of climax and was impaled in a manner that he had so many times done to so many women. The queen was sorry to have lost such a worthy companion, but she knew that she would surely find another. The king returned to his mercantile ways and gathered much gold.

All things that were happening were of interest to an unwanted observer. Furbaide sat with his eyes closed, but this time he was not alone. He was watching and telling all that he saw to his new found prize. Though not even a year old, Kieiran was full grown. The curse had given him not only the animal look, but also the growth rate. "My boy, what I have seen tells me that we will soon be paid a visit from The Hound. I am sure you would like to have the powers of Cuchulainn and even though he will probably be a little on the tough side he should make a tasty meal."

Kieiran's hair-covered face moved from the darkness into his father's sight. "I am looking forward to this fine meal, father." The drool ran down the chin and off the hair that came to a point, as his pointed teeth gleemed in the thought of taking the powers given to Cuchulainn.

# 6
# Rebuilding the Old War Machine

The time was drawing near when the icebridge would open a path that would link the islands together. In the times of old when the island had been one with the land of the Great Forest, all people were in touch in some manner or the other. Tribes would wander over the land masses to trade and some to take what others had gathered. Those who had been left on the islands in the sky, did not have much contact due to the water that had flooded after the great thaw in the age of ice. Alba had been populated by nothing but raiders. They had come by way of the north seas and from what is now known as Spain. They were not farmers and lived mostly by hunting as well as taking what they needed from those who did farm. Mostly red-haired or blonde, they had brought the Celtic features to these isles. To invade the lands of these warlike people was to ask for massive slaughter, for dying was a trip to the world of the pagan gods where warriors lived as kings.

Cuchulainn was aware of what the cost would be and so were the generals of the Ulster army. They had to prepare and make plans to use a different style of fighting but still remain with honor.

Emain Macha was more like its old self now that they had good leaders. Their pride was back and The Hound had left a well-respected general to run the city as it had been run before. Celtchar mac Uthidir had once killed a thousand invaders from the north sea. He was forced to hold a gate while whores that were sent to the city by the invaders had poisoned his relief. He closed one side of the gate to narrow the passage and after a prayer to Smertrios, he had stood for ten hours and fought without help or water. He stood on a mound of bodies that formed a wall to slow down his enemies advance. His need for water became so great that he began to drink the blood of those that he had killed. His wounds were terrible and sleep was his worst enemy. The Norsemen waited until he began to nod off then they attacked in force. Smertrios looked on this brave warrior with respect and sent the glowing ring that gave him strength and took away the sleep problem. He looked to the Norsemen, who were making their last charge, and began to sing the praises of Smertrios. As the horde neared the gate they heard his song.

Let me sing of myself and glory I will hold,
My thanks I do dispose to Smertrios,
for making me so bold,
Norsemen's blood I do spill, in His holy name,
Let my sword do his work and bathe in the fame,
Hear me as I sing, to this last refrain,
And know that I kill you without a hint of shame,
Breath you deep of the air that you dare invade,
Knowing well that it's you last,
for death is in my blade,
So come you hordes to this gate
that I know so well,
For I am here to do my work
and send you all to hell.

In the hour that followed, he sent three hundred

Norsemen to their graves. The rest turned and retreated to their boats and sailed away never to return.

Celtcha had done the task that Cuchulainn had left him to do. He had returned Emain Macha to a place of order and was in the process of rebuilding the army that had melted in the surrounding fields and glenns of Ulster. Of this The Hound was very happy and gave Celtcha a place of honor in his ranks.

The time to march was nearing and Cuchulainn was pleased with his war machine. His leaders were blessed with many gifts of the gods. Gwydion had the night vision and the invisible spear, Mac Roth could hear and smell as good as any fox in the isle, Adian, although not well practiced, could cast his magic at will, Gavyn was blessed with his father's knowledge of tact and gile in battle, and also could send a spear for long distances with deadly results, and of course Celtcha, whose courage and relations with the god of war were self-evident.

It was time to gather warriors and supplies. This would be easy, for all those in Ulster loved their warrior hero. All that he asked was done with great haste. Supplies began to show up daily. Warriors would walk from the far reaches of Ulster. Some from the farms brought the weapons of their trade.

They showed up with the weapons they fought with daily to break the soil and grow crops. Some came with their oldest sons, but most left a son at home to tend the farm. All men of Ulster were warriors at heart and the farmers looked forward to having a chance to do battle . . . and also to get away from their wives. Emain Macha was a busy place. All the townspeople were making carts and weapons. Women were weaving the tartans of Ulster so that each warrior could be distinguished in the midst of battle. Arrows were being made by the thousands, for

71

Cuchulainn had battle plans that were different than the normal frontal charge. The Hound would tell no one of his plans for he feared the long vision which he knew Furbaide was surely putting to good use. Food was being stockpiled in large amounts. The main source of the supplies were grains that lasted for long periods of time and could be prepared in cakes to be carried by each warrior. All meats and vegetables were being dried. The carts were being built to carry these sources of life to the army as well as live food sources, such as chickens, ducks, and rabbits. Cattle and pigs would be driven along with the troops.

In these times there were several levels of fighters. The first level were the foot soldiers, mostly made up of low social orders, people that hoped to gain status by being brave and successful in battle. They also profited from looting and enjoyed the rape and pillage that was part of their payment. The next level was made up of young warriors that have proven themselves in battle or are the sons of chieftains and officers in the ranks. They made up the cavalry and were used as the second force after the charge. They were little more than foot soldiers on horse back. The third level were experienced warriors and chieftains of the different tribes that filled Ulster's population. It was not uncommon for these warriors to run to the front of the battle lines to challenge the top warriors of the enemy to have one-on-one battle. They would strip off all their clothes, carrying only their weapons, expecting divine protection. They would call to their enemies and taunt them with songs, insults to their lineage, and then boast loudly what they had done to former enemies as well as what they were about to do to them. Nobles and the high-ranking families made the final ranks. They came in chariots with drivers who were masters at their trade. It was up to them to deliver the nobles to the front at the proper time to take credit for the success of their troops or hurry them away in defeat. These were the well-dressed combatants. Adorned with as much gold as they could stand up with and fancy designs on bronze breastplates topped off with horned helmets of bronze. Their weapons were more for show than battle. Jewels and gold covered the grip and most had carved Celtic designs in the blades. This was easily done because bronze was a soft metal. Aboard each chariot was a steel sword to do combat with, not so pretty but strong enough to remove heads or limbs. They had several throwing spears as well as two stabbing spears. These spears were the weapons of choice in that they kept the enemy at a distance and both ends could be used in a close fight. Archers were not common in the ranks during this period of time because the bow of the day was not designed for distance and the arrows lost effect after so many yards. Instead there were several hundred missile throwers who used slings with sharp-edged rocks that were broken to create a cutting wound and give a warrior much discomfort.

Along with the soldiers came an assortment of camp followers. The most revered were the camp whores. They wanted to be there when the pillage and looting began and were known to issue credit to those who would pay them from the booty soon to be theirs. Out of need and respect of the profession, payment was usually made firsthand after the looting was finished. Slave traders from all over showed up to buy anyone that was in one piece after the battle. They came with both sides and kept their distance from the battlefields. They could not afford to support one side, for they bid on any prospects taken by the winning side. Both sides tolerated them. Cooks, blacksmiths, entertainers, and druids came along to invoke the gods to support their side. Druids were the most important followers because the active gods of the Celts were a fickle lot and needed constant praise. The druids had descended from the oldest of the settlers on these isles. From the sky, in times past, came people of the fairest of skin and blonde hair. They arrived in a ball of fire that landed on the tops of several mountains. They had knowledge and skills that no others possessed. They soon became the spiritual leaders of not only the people of the isles, but also the land of the Great Forest.

The time had come to march on the dreaded dark ones of Alba and bring back the honor that had been stolen by Furbaide Fer Benn.

# 7
# The Gods and Who They Support

Deity was an important part of the Celtic pagan life. Each god dealt with the Celts on a daily basis. If the winds blew hard on a bright summer day and the smell of flowers happened to enter a Celt's nostrils, it was a gift from Nantosuelta, goddess of nature. If the god of thunder, Taranis, called out in his rumbling voice, it could be a warning to get to high ground for swells of water could be close behind. Belennus was god of sunlight, Belisama, goddess of light and fire. The two most respected were Cernunnos and Ogmios. The druids were in constant contact with Ogmios. He helped them with their intellect and gave them a special language all their own. Cernunnos was the horned god that had put the curse on Kieran. Maybe it was not meant as a terrible curse since this god ruled over the animals, wealth, fertility and the underworld.

It was not unusual for the gods to intervene in the lives of special mortals. The Greek gods played games with the lives of their followers and so the practice was not so unusual. They would meet in glenns of the countryside where fairies, gnomes, elves, trolls, and certain monsters lived in another dimension. The forest turned an emerald green when the gods went to their meeting place, fluffy pink lined clouds would gather to form the roof. Animals were allowed to sit close by and listen to the gods of nature. A huge tree stump provided the meeting table. Large amounts of fruit, cheese and bread adorned the table. Unlike the mortals, the gods drank nectar and fresh wine but never ate meat.

As the gods and goddesses began to sit around the table, it was noticeable that there was no head to the table because no one god ruled over another. Each had a responsibility to uphold in the realm of nature. They each said their greetings and then the business at hand was brought forth.

There was about to be a major fight that would involve all the gods and the mortals. Cernunnos spoke first, "Who here supports The Hound of Ulster in his return to leadership of the men that lost their courage?" About half raised their hands to show their support. This was a surprise to the animal god, he had hoped that most of the gods would be on his side. "Alright then, give to him the gifts you have to give. I will continue to favor the camp of the men of Alba, for they amuse me more."

Danu spoke, "Why do you support such a rabble of human waste?"

"Oh, I see that my beauty has feelings for The Hound of Ulster,"cited the horned one.

"It's not a matter of feelings, it is a matter of right and wrong."

"And what do you mean by that statement?"

"The invasion of Ulster was an affront to the rules of war. Furbaide took advantage of the fact that Conchobor was recently returned from the great battle and his troops were exhausted. He sent a message that he had come to honor the victory of Ulster and was received as a friend."

"All that you say is true, but it is in the past, we must now consider who to support in the up and coming battle," said Cernunnos. "I choose to stay with the men of Alba and my new warrior that will give notice to the world soon."

"I too will support them," sang out Teutates.

"The smart ass Hound killed my only pet and I have been very lonely since."

"Count me in to help the raiders of Alba," shouted Taranis, god of thunder.

Rosmerta and Danu stood together in support of Cuchulainn. They were joined by the goddess Nantosuelta, who was at odds with Eagon. Belisama, Ogmios, Epona, and Belenus decided to stay neutral. The lesser gods made no commitments to either side. The lines were now drawn with the gods and the lines of battle were soon to be drawn with the mortals.

# 8
# The Trap

The gods had made their choices, but it was still up to the mortals to do what they do best and that was kill. Cuchulainn led the army of five thousand to the icebridge and started to cross. Taranis still was mad at the loss of his green slime pet, and had been working on another plan to stop the advance. He had contact with other monsters that lived in the waters that the Ulster men were crossing. This was a more formidable creature and the god hoped that The Hound would be more impressed by his newfound pet.

Seven warriors that could take charge at any time now surrounded The Hound. Cuchulainn was hoping that one would step forward and take the leadership from him. He had never wanted to be king or to take over the leadership of these men. He was the master of warfare and this was good enough for him. He had determined that the warrior who came forward and showed the best leader qualities would earn the long vision, and the throne of Ulster.

The human chain of warriors and their baggage was a sight to behold. They sang songs of past victories and were of good cheer. In the evenings, large pots of stew and bread were consumed around gleaming campfires. Of course they also drank ale from horn cups that were used in battle to frighten their enemies when blown. The sound of more than a thousand horns made a strange wailing sound noise that sounded like banshees screaming though the air.

It was always like this before a battle. Men who had not fought before were sure that they would be the bravest of all, and they hoped to be noticed by their leaders. They pictured themselves covered in gold ornaments and women, which the leaders would bestow on the most furious warriors. The older and more experienced combatants were of a different mind. They had survived battle and had no plans to put their lives on the line for glory. It was the bounty of the pillaging that they wanted to fight for and the pleasures of running down a fleeing enemy and wreaking havoc in blood lust killing. The top line warriors were here to enjoy the legends that would be sung about their great feats in battle. The bards and druids made sure that this would happen, for it was to their benefit to have favor with the chieftains and kings.

It was the last night of the crossing on the icebridge. Cuchulainn and his newfound companions were camped in the middle of the circular encampment in case there might be an attack; they would have time to respond. The stew was of lamb, which seemed to be a favorite of the top line warriors, and the ale was spiked with honey. All was good and conversation was even better. Gavyn, in his state of mindless youth and out of pure curiosity, asked a question of Gwydion that all would have asked if it had not been in such bad taste. "Gwydion, how did you manage to give birth to such beautiful daughters?" All present froze as if they were turned to stone. Silence was so thick that there was doubt that Cuchulainn's sword could have cut through it.

Surprisingly, her response was quite civil. The reason why was not real clear because she had slit throats for much less offensive questions. The fact that Bridget and young Gavyn were very much in love could have been the reason, or maybe she realized that teenagers sometimes speak out without any thought of the consequences. Anyway, she seemed mellowed by the evening and the honeyed ale. "I must tell you the truth, these lovely visions are not of my womb. Finian the fair one had a wife before me, she died giving birth to Bridget. He knew that the girls would need to grow up strong and able to defend themselves. I was a warrior in the ranks before anyone knew I was a woman. I won my honors by proving myself in battle after battle. I married a fair maiden in the guise that I was a man, needless to say, it was not long before I was found out. Cathbad, my wife, was happy with me as I was and we had a happy life together. On a summer's evening we were swimming in the stream at Glenn Lochnar. Cathbar was a lovely sight to my eyes. A large woman and strong of mind and heart, she met my needs.

"On this evening, there was a young warrior from the village that came to the stream to wash himself. My love had fallen asleep just before the young man entered the creek. I had seen many men naked while in the ranks, but none so fair as this young bull. I began to feel my body grow warm and I knew I must sample this ripe melon. As you can see, I am no beauty and I feared that if I approached him as a woman, he might run away. Once again in the guise of a man I approached him. He was quick to grab his spear and challenge me. Then he saw who I was and knew I lived in the outskirts of the village. We sat down and started to talk, he was indeed fair and he liked the company of men. This gave me even more of a challenge. Soon we were in each other's embraces. I prayed to sheela-na-gig, my look-alike, for her help. I needed this one as a woman. We soon went past the point of no return and it didn't matter to either of us what gender the other preferred. As we both rolled in the throes of sex, I felt his body wrench forward and I was sure it was my sexual presence that conquered this young buck. But it was not ecstasy that made him jerk; it was the sharpness of his spear as it entered his back and heart. I pushed him aside and saw Cathbad draw the spear's edge across her neck. All I saw was the blood of my love and the blood of my lust pouring into the stream. To get this off my mind I joined the ranks of Finian just before the Tain'. No longer did I disguise my womanhood. Finian offered me his home if I would raise his daughters as warriors. So mother I am, but of blood kin I am not. Let there be no mistake, I love these two girls as my own."

Moved by the tale of the evening, all slowly slid under the skins that kept the chill from their bodies. All were anxious for the next day to come, for they would complete the crossing of the icebridge and would be on the soil of the dark ones. As the campfires began to burn low, a strange green light covered the ice and snow. Under this, ice movement could be seen. The warriors that were on guard-duty began to feel uneasy and went to the spots in the ice where the movement could be seen. They looked at each other baffled. Just then through the ice burst two water serpents. The guards threw down their spears and ran screaming toward the middle of the camp.

In another dimension, the god Taranis laughed and turned to his fellow conspirators, "Let's see if The Hound has an answer for my two new pets." The other gods giggled with glee at the discomfort their friend had dished out to Cuchulainn.

The dragonlike creatures began to move through the camp feasting on sleeping Ulster men and women. The sound of crunching bones and screams woke The Hound, who grabbed his sword and stabbing spear. The other warriors were startled by the cries for help and the devastating sounds of people dying. The Hound ran from the center of the camp toward the strange sounds made by the serpents. To his dismay there are two problems to deal with, both sea serpents were feasting on warrior after warrior. Cuchulainn and Gavyn, each took a serpent to do battle with.

From the depths of the ocean these creatures had been summoned by Taranis. They were scale-covered, which gave them a well-protected plate of armor on their breast and back. A feeding frenzy had drawn them to what resembled a school of fish, which was their normal diet. The warriors were much easier to catch and had more meat to satisfy their appetites. They slithered on their bellies instead of walking or crawling and could raise their heads as does a cobra.

Cuchulainn was joined by Adain and Celtcha. Gwydion and her daughters ran to support Gavyn. As the other warriors began to gather their wits, they too grabbed weapons and advanced to the battle. The serpents seemed to slither faster on the ice and this made it hard to get close enough to deliver any meaningful blows. The battle was not going good for the men of Ulster, and the monsters from the deep were consuming many.

The goddess Danu looked through her magic pool of spring-water. She saw the struggle that was taking place and realized that The Hound was not the best when it came to tactics. She decided to intervene once again to provide Cuchlainn with what he needed.

The Hound was throwing spears at the raised chest of the massive creature. This was producing little results other than making the serpent mad. Its head lunged forward and the great jaws slammed shut incasing the body of another brave warrior. Blood flew all over The Hound and his companions. Once again Cuchulainn advanced with his sword and attempted to stab the creature. Celtcha was by his side with his mighty axe and swung with great force in hopes of penetrating the armor plate. This too was not effective and turned the monster's attention to the two small annoying fleas that bit at the serpent's chest. The serpent slid forward and knocked both warriors backwards near the place where Adian was standing in a support position. The young magician could be of little help, for his magic was still limited to tricks and also he could only be effective on mortals. He reached down to help The Hound and Celtcha to their feet, "What might I do to help?"

"You best stay clear and run for more help," shouted Cuchulainn.

The other warriors were faring no better. The four of them had surrounded the monster and dodged in and out inflicting what harm they might. Gavyn's strategy was good and seemed to confuse this beast from hell. The scales were preventing the serpents from suffering very much harm. Gavyn saw the head of the monster move in Bridget's direction, so with a great leap he jumped onto its neck and this drew the attention away from his teenage love. She saw that her companion had put himself in great danger on her behalf. The serpent did its best to unseat this brave youngster, but he held fast. As all of this was taking place, Danu leaned toward the water pool and thought, *What would these monsters fear the most?* As she pondered, she thought of the only thing that all men feared the most. Just maybe these creatures might react in the same manner.

She raised her hands into the air and cried, "Awake damsel warriors!" She knew that it was the cleansing time for the troops of Gwydion's women warriors and nothing could stand against their fury. Also, it was not good to wake them in the middle of the night for they would be twice as cranky. As they arose from sleep to the sound of battle, they were prepared for anything. They gathered up their swords and spears and charged toward the two monsters.

The screeching voices, bulging eyes, and look of a furious desire to hurt someone really bad was all it took to run the sea serpents back to the holes from which they had attacked. On this night, man or monster could not match these two hundred cranky women. Cuchulainn walked to the lady warrior that had led the charge and thanked her for the help. "Help, my ass, if it had not been for us you would have been serpent shit in about a day," screeched Tuala.

"Well, I am sure we could have handled it," said The Hound.

"Bullshit, you were about to be eaten and that's all I have to say. Except, your man ass let about a hundred warriors be eaten and I guess you would have let them eat us in our sleep if someone hadn't given us the alarm.

"Now Tuala, we didn't wake you ladies because Gwydion said it would be a big mistake not to let you get your rest."

"Goddamn, you idiot, if we had been eaten in our sleep, it really wouldn't have made any damn difference, would it?" The lady warriors turned and walked to their encampment. "What the hell did I say to set her off like that?" questioned The Hound.

"Damned if I know," said Gavyn.

In Furbaide's castle things were beginning to look up. He had seen that over a hundred warriors had been taken away from the strength of Cuchulainn's army. His daughters were sitting next to their newfound brother who had settled into this family quite well. They enjoyed brushing the hair on his cheeks and laughed when he howled as the brush hung on a hair knot. He never got mad at the girls because they would bring him some really good snacks after they had their little torture sessions with the captives from raids.

"Father?"

"Yes, my son."

"How soon will it be before I get my new powers from Cuchlainn?" growled Kieiran.

"Son, The Hound enters Alba tomorrow."

"But he is still two days away from our fort, Father."

"Again, you are correct, but I have a little surprise for the mighty one. It may take some of the wind out of his sails, Ha Ha Ha," laughed the king.

All of the troops in the Ulster force had cleared the ice-bridge and were once again on solid ground. Cuchulainn was familiar with the land of Alba, he had gone there to get his warrior training. He had traveled from west to east and was given special skills from the prophetess Scathach. He stood in battle with her sons against the army of Aife, the greatest of female chieftains at this time. Aife had challenged Scathach to combat on the rope of feats; Cuchulainn asked to take her place and she accepted. The Hound's skills were not well-honed and it looked as if he would be defeated when his sword broke off at the hilt. The Hound was aware of Aife's love for her horses; charioteer and chariot. He tricked her by saying that he could see all three and they had been killed, when she turned to look, he grabbed her by her tits and threw her over his shoulder. He threatened her life if she did not give him three wishes. One wish was for her to leave

Scathach alone, to sleep with him, and for her to give him a child.

These memories were in the mind of The Hound as he drove deeper into Alba. As he rode with his companions, he made a decision, "Adain, it is time for you to take on a new place for me. I will be in need of a loyal brave chariot driver and you have proven yourself all that I need." Adian was shaken by this great honor and stood speechless for a minute. All that rode close by raised their voices in a salute to the young warrior for this was a tribute to his skills as well as his loyalty. Adian spoke, "I will accept this responsibility and The Hound will have no one more ready to die for him." This pleased everyone and raised their spirits to the highest levels.

Furbaide's surprise was soon to be revealed. He had sent Eagon and his son, Noishu, to plan an ambush. He sent his special forces to make hit and run attacks in hopes of cutting into the strength of the Ulster men. His purpose was to break the courage of Cuchulainn's forces; what he did not know was that The Hound and Gavyn had expected just such action and had prepared a little surprise of their own.

Cuchulainn had been impressed with Gavyn's long arms that could sling a spear longer than the strongest of warriors. He had met with the teenager late at night and together they designed a new bow and arrow that had killer force at a long distance. No one was allowed to speak of this new weapon for fear of the long vision that belonged to the king of the dark ones.

As the column entered the valley before the last road that led to Furbaide's fort, the sound of wailing war horns began. The forest became alive with naked warriors on foot, on horseback, and in war chariots. They did give some surprise and of course the surprise set fear in the

Ulster men who had been so badly defeated by these savages once before. The Albans attacked from both sides in full frontal force. It was the traditional way and The Hound had hoped for this method to be used.

Gavyn turned to Cuchulainn and asked, *"Now?"*

*"Now,* cried The Hound. Gavyn pointed to Celtcha, who pulled his horn and let go with a mighty blow. When the sound was heard in the ranks, all the warriors pulled back near the wagons which were side by side as far as the eye could see.

From the hillside, Eagon turned to Noishu, "The cowards are in full retreat."

"Yes, father," smiled the young warrior. "Let us attack in full force and finish this now."

"Indeed if they have no heart for battle then we could finish off the Ulster men once and for all." An old druid priest stepped forward to speak with Eagon, "Beware of The Hound, he is known for his great warrior ways and this does indeed seem strange for him to withdraw."

"Victory is within our grasp and you need to prepare for prayers to the gods for our victory," smirked Noishu.

"Then let it be," said the druid.

It was then that Eagon turned to the forces that were there to perform the raids of hit and run, and waved them into the battle. Their horses snorted as the heels of the riders urged them to spring into the attack. Two thousand horses and screaming men burst from the forest following the foot soldiers in their head long charge.

The men of Ulster were ready to meet this attack in their usual manner, but the word had been given late in the night to preform as they were doing. They did not like this but they had great trust in The Hound and no one would disobey his orders.

As the mass of Alban warriors were now running at

full speed, the gap closed to within a hundred yards. The Hound had sent his leaders to stand with their tribes and/or troops. He was in the middle so his horn could be heard by all the Ulster men and women. He raised the horn to his lips and blew with all his might. At the sound, the covers over the wagons were thrown back to reveal three ranks of bowmen facing each way. Each had the strange new weapon in his hand, and the long bows were drawn and ready. The work done in Emain Macha was about to be tested. Iron tips gleamed on the arrows and the shafts were longer and balanced. The horn sounded again, and as the foot soldiers stood in position to protect the archers. It was then that the first flight of arrows went sailing into the mass of charging dark ones.

On this day, warfare would never be the same, as the birth of the long bow took place. Warriors dropped like shafts of wheat as the second round of arrows fell like rain from hell. The field of battle was a carpet of bodies and the ranks that charged from the back lines were forced to step on dead and dying comrades in order to maintain the attack. Then came the third round of death from the glimmering blue sky. Screams of pain could be heard on the mountainside where the general stood in disbelief at what was taking place. He had faced archers and missile throwers in many battles, but they had only been effective at close range and a charge so bold would continue through the fray. As the raiders neared the attack lines, Eagon could hear screams of a different type. When the first rank of archers reloaded to send a second round of arrows, the riders were within range of the mighty bow. A thousand arrows were let loose, soon followed by another thousand. The sound of the cries of pain—that of the warriors and their loyal mounts, was so strange to the ear that even the gods stopped and listened.

Cernunnos had to turn away when he saw his gallant horses kicking in dying throws. His heart was very heavy and he knew he must stop the killing now. With little haste, he began to cry. His tears fell with such force that the arrows could not fly straight enough to have the killing force.

The help came too late for those of Alba. More than half their army was gone and most of what was left had at least taken one arrow. Cuchulainn raised his hand to stop the archers. All the warriors stood up in silence and looked upon the field where lay their most dreaded enemy. There was little movement among the mass of death. The new weapon was mightier than the dragon's teeth, and much more deadly. Normally this was the time to chase the foes in defeat and disgrace them, defile their women and take heads as trophies of a great victory. No-one moved among the Ulster men.

They looked to one another for some pride, but there was none to claim in this battle. No blood on their weapons, no wounded; not one Ulster man had died. Celtcha moved close to The Hound, "Where is the pride in this great warrior?"

Slowly turning to the old warrior, a stunned Cuchulainn said,"I never expected this. I only wanted to give us the edge due to their numbers. Never have I seen such killing. Are there no Albans just wounded?"

The mighty seven looked to the battlefield, there was no movement. Only the crows and ravens had come to begin their feast. That was all the movement that could be seen.

On the hilltop, about a hundred Alban warriors set on their horses in silence. Their eyes were glazed over in disbelief and their hearts were in their stomachs. Sons, brothers, fathers, and uncles of the survivors all lay dead in a storm of arrows.

Eagon looked to Noishu, "Go to the fort and report what has happened here today."

"But father, I cannot take this news to Furbaide, he will draw and quarter me."

"Alright, send Car, he is low rank and he will not take out his anger on him.

"I will follow with the rest and make all known to the king. We will now have to prepare for the siege on the fort."

As usual, the camp followers went among the dead and gathered up all the booty they could carry. The birds that prey on the dead were there in force. They seemed to like to gather up the eyeballs first. Some wounded were forced to suffer the pain of having their eyes removed by these rude surgeons.

The slave merchants were not happy with the results of such a complete kill. They gathered in a meeting to confront Cuchulainn with their complaints. There was an Etruscan who fancied himself leader of these human scavengers, and he felt a complaint should be leveled on The Hound.

"You have cheated us out of our take in this battle. There are but a few alive and they may be destined to death. This new style of killing is too complete, you must change your new method of slaughter or we will all be out of business." The Hound sat among his fellow warriors having ale and bread. He looked at this seller of slaves with little respect, yet he knew there could be a time he might need them. Therefore, he tried to hold back his anger at this scum that had the balls to condemn a method of battle that had saved him probably one to two thousand warriors' lives.

"You have come to serve only the winning side on this war and I do not think you have the right to condemn my actions," said The Hound with as much restraint as he could muster.

Domitius, the Etruscan, spoke again in a demanding manner,"You must not change the rules of war as we know it."

"We are all here to gain from each other and you will be glad to take my gold and silver for slaves when the battles end."

"True, you piece of cow dung, but I do not take a tongue lashing from the likes of you," shouted The Hound as he jumped to his feet. Drawing his dagger, he grabbed the merchant by his hair, lifting him from the ground and slowly removing his head. The slave buyer could see the face of the enraged Cuchulainn and then he saw nothing. It's not a good idea to enrage such a mighty warrior.

As the camp of the men of Ulster was settling down, the eyes of Furbaide were focused on what had happened this day. He opened his eyes and a terrible scream resounded through the fortress. The door opened and Kieran ran in followed by Rian who was assigned as the flesh eaters guardian. "Father what has happened?"

"This bastard's father has lost half our army on this, the first attack."

"But sir, this cannot be, for my father is the finest battle master in all of Alban," said Rian.

"Well he just lost that title to The Hound of Ulster."

"Father, what will we do now?" quizzed Kieran.

"Well, the first thing is we will teach Eagon a lesson in what happens when one fails in this kingdom."

"Yes father, what is this lesson?"

Furbaide called out to the guards to come forward. As they approached the king, he motioned for them to grab Rian. He looked at his monster-son and asked, "When have you last eaten?" A smile came to the hair-covered face and the long pointed teeth glistened in the darkness of the room. His father was going to once again give him the pleasure of a blood feast. Furbaide called to the queen and his daughters to come and witness what was about to happen. As they entered the room and took their places beside their father, he gave a small flick of the wrist to unleash the horror of Alba.

Rian realized what was about to happen, and then he remembered the night the god Cernunnos took the child, and when he returned with a skull that looked like him. The young warrior pulled away from one of the guards, drew his sword then killed him. The other guard leaped onto Rian's back, in an effort to bring him to the ground, but was thrown to the feet of the king. Rian lunged forward and shoved his sword into the face of the guard, who bellowed out in pain and fell dead. Rian then looked up into the eyes of the king and jumped forward in an attempt to finish him. When he came forward he felt a terrible pain in his stomach as a large spear blade began its work at hand. Kieran had stopped the charge and now had the pleasure of raising the handsome young warrior in the air, impaled. He would not go easily and took a swing with his sword at the animal man. Blood began to run down the shaft and as it ran on to the arms of the monster he indulged himself and licked at the flowing red wine. Kieran had the strength and senses of all the predators, and held Rian aloft until his sisters could come to his assistance. They waited till the beautiful blonde warrior dropped his weapon to the floor and then they began to rip at the muscular arms, tearing away small pieces of flesh, feeding the tidbits to their brother. Rian grew weak as his lifeblood was draining from his body. He called out in his loudest cry to Noishu and Eagon, "Beware the monster and his father."

Noishu was on the road to the fortress when he felt the spear enter his twin brother's bowels. He knew then that his brother was in the throes of death. They had always fought as one and he felt the pain of not dying at his brother's side. He took heed of his brother's warning and turned his horse around and rode back to Eagon.

Eagon had heard the warning as well in a vision. He knew that his son had died in battle and would enter the underworld with his best armor and weapons. There he would be received as a warrior and would have many beautiful women, eat the finest meats and have a neverending flow of ale. Eagon felt the pain of a father who had lost a son, yet he was bound by honor to return to the fort and take his punishment for failing. This time, he was going with hatred, instead of fear.

In the camp of the Ulster men there was much dissent, for the battle they had come for had not happened. Cuchulainn had given orders to lay seige to the fort and start raiding the countryside for food and slaves to keep the camp in order. This relieved some of the tension, also he had troops assigned to groups surrounding the fort in case the Alban men would come out to test their strength or try and take food. The Hound was not good at this kind of warfare and was now sorry that Gavyn had talked him into using this new weapon.

Gavyn could tell that things were not good in the camp. He had his father's skills for warfare and leadership. His fighting skills were not up to the standards of the great warriors, but he was well-liked by the chieftains and the officers of rank. The kingly approach to common

95

problems and his lighthearted manner could lift all those around him to great heights. He was a leader of men as well as an understanding judge of the faults of most men. He had courage which he showed in battle. He often got himself in trouble by taking chances to prove to the men that he was not too good to fight in the front lines.

He had his father's lust for women and had spent many nights showing his bedside manner to the royal ladies. But now his heart lusted for only one creature, Bridget. Each day he watched her grow in all the womanly ways. She had been tall, like a stalk of corn, but now like that very stalk she was growing large buds. Her hips were rounding into powerful round mounds that were firm and enticing. Her breasts were not at full bloom, but were beginning to balance out enough to offer a most interesting subject for young Gavyn to study. Her looks only added to the package that he had loved the day she entered his father's hut.

The night was cold in this dark place and no one was in comfort as the wind cut through the skins and heavily woven wools that clothed them. The fire burned high and supplied some relief. Gavyn sat next to Bridget as he had in his father's house and listened as she told the stories that had been so much enjoyment to Fergus. He looked into her eyes and watched the fire reflection dance on the surface of the sky-blue pools. His chest began to heave and his manhood had become aroused. He wished that on this night he might take this young lamb for his own. As his mind wandered with sexual thoughts, he turned to look straight into the eyes of Gwydion and knew that all his hopes would not happen this night. His thoughts suddenly changed directions and he said to himself, "Damn that woman is ugly."

He rose and moved near The Hound, who was sitting

back from the fire. Adian, the old one, Mac Roth, and Celtcha were there with him. The Hound was deep into the ale this night and it was not a real good time to bring up any sensible conversation, but youth does not take this sort of thing into consideration. "Cuchulainn, why are you getting drunk?" asked Gavyn.

"Me getting drunk?" barked The Hound, "There is not enough ale in all of Alba to get me drunk. Bring me another horn full right now."

"My good friend, have you forgotten what happened to you the last time you got drunk?" asked Mac Roth.

"Yeh," quipped Adian. "The next day, you were ready to kill yourself."

The Hound closed one eye and tried to focus on Gwydion.

"Ha, Ha, Hey beautiful baby, do you want to try and wrestle The Hound one more time."

"You drunken pig, you have forgotten that I am the best you have ever had. At least, that's what you said that night."

Gavyn saw his chance to be alone with Bridget and he entered the conversation one more time.

"Dear Cuchulainn, maybe you were not the best Gwydion ever had. Have you thought about that?" Gulping down the ale and reaching for one more, The Hound spoke in a blurred manner, "This woman could nebber had no man as good in bett as I."

"Hound, you were as a child and I made you a man that night," teased Gwydion.

"That's enough come to me and see dis manhood in my pants."

Gwydion rose to her feet and went to The Hound. She looked down at him, "Let's see it big bold warrior."

97

"Okay." The Hound tried to stand up and fell into the hairy arms of the warrior princess.

"Dib you seez it?"

"Well, not yet, but I will soon." As she helped him toward her tent, in a last show for his friends, Cuchulainn grabbed her by the butt and gave a big wink.

Mac Roth laid his hand on that of Adian, "Well young charioteer, it sounds like our fearless leader is going to do it again." Small amounts of laughter could be heard as The Hound disappeared into the tent of Gwydion.

The two young ones had one more obstacle, a sister. As they joined hands a third hand grabbed them both. They turned to see Morrigan standing with a serious look on her face; it faded to a soft smile. "You two go to my tent, but you must be gentle with my sister. If you hurt her, I will kill you." They slipped away from the fire as all the others were having a laugh at the expense of The Hound. Morrigan's tent was covered with skins of sheep and a large bear rug which Morrigan had killed at age eight. It was warm and soft. The two laid down side by side and turned to kiss, just then Morrigan's face appeared at the skin flap door, "I will guard for you, but I ask only one favor."

"What is the favor, dear sister?" asked Bridget.

"Only that I will be next to have your warrior." That was the way of the Celts.

In the fortress of the dark ones, Furbaide watched the things that were going on in the camp of The Hound. He too had discontent from the warriors that were led by Eagon. He questioned his own actions and thought that maybe he had made a fatal mistake. Eagon was in the fort but he and Noishu had not come to the hut of the king. This made Furbaide a little uncomfortable, and he decided to call on divine help. His druids were called to his fortress and he doubled the guard. The guards were told not to let anyone in the royal fort without the king's approval, especially Eagon. The druids were told to search for help from the gods. Furbaide's army had been cut in half, yet he still had a formidable force of well-tested warriors. The king felt that he had lost the support of these excellent killers and he was right, for they loved their leader, Eagon.

The king decided to call for Eagon and his remaining son to come before him. Still a brave warrior and loyal to Alban, Eagon accepted the king's call. His most loyal officers told him to be aware of the situation and do not trust anything that Furbiade laid in front of him. His anger was his moving force but he needed an answer as to the death of his son, Rian.

The druids were busy trying to make contact with the gods and especially Cernunnos. They were committing several captured warriors to human sacrifice by fire. A large fire was built in the middle of the king's hut. The captured men and women were wrapped in wicker baskets and rolled onto the blazing flames. They soon were consumed in the rolling waves of fire. Their screams gave comfort to the royal family who so loved to witness pain of the helpless. Soon one of the druid priests fell to the ground and slowly he turned into the image of the great god Cernunnos. He stood in front of the king; his horns dripping with blood and death smelled to the high heavens.

"Why have you called me up from my rest?" asked the god. Somewhat taken aback by this apparition, the king responded, "I have need of your help, oh great god of the underworld," cried Furbaide. This was a good approach to the gods, for they were very vain and enjoyed praise, whether or not it was sincere. "I have been your loyal servant and faithful supplier of human offerings."

"Then of course, you are looking for a favor from me in return, correct?" asked this god.

"Great Cernunnos, I only ask that you direct me in the correct manner of battle to defeat this Hound of Ulster."

"What is wrong with a straightforward frontal attack?" inquired the god.

"Thanks to the decision of my general we have lost one half of our forces and our enemy has a weapon that we cannot equal."

"Gather your troops and make them ready for the great and honorable frontal attack, I will take care of the rest."

"But what will I do with my general, Eagon?"

"Call him to you and beg for his forgiveness and then honor him with a one-on-one battle against Cuchulainn; he will either honor you or die. After the battle, send your warriors forward and I will introduce you to the power of the god of the animals and the underworld."

All things in the fort returned to normal. The druids left and the remains of the sacrifice were taken to the backroom where the son and daughters of Furbaide feasted on the remains. The king motioned to his guards to allow Eagon and Noishu to come into his presence. "Come forward dear general, so that I might give you my deepest regrets on the untimely death of your son, Rian. He was a great and loyal prince whom I will miss as if he were my own."

"I do not have time for this kind of talk, just tell me what happened to my boy."

"He died with honor, protecting me from an assassin, who came in with the suppliers of food."

"His loyalty will be honored at his funeral pyre, for he fought like a madman in my defense."

"Were it not for Rian and my son, I would surely be dead at this moment."

Eagon came near the throne of the king, "I have not heard the details until now my king."

"All I ask is that his body be returned to me and his brother, so that we may give him a proper burial."

"Unfortunately, we were forced to burn his remains in the warrior way and there is nothing left but his ashes," said the king. "Now, enough of this talk of those who are in a better place."

"We have need of your courage to make up for your mistake in battle."

"You will challenge The Hound in single combat, and if you win, the men of Ulster will no longer have a leader."

"I will do this thing, but not for you. This will be in honor of Rian."

"Good then, let the war horns sound and call the great Cuchulainn from his encampment to do battle," said Furbaide.

# 9

# The Final Battle

The sun rose on the grass and snow carpet. The hut of
Cuchulainn was warm with a nice morning fire burning
and the smell of hog fat frying potatoes left over from the
night before. Mac Roth and the young magician sat near
the flames warming themselves. At a short distance, they
saw the massive outline of The Hound walking slowly toward them. He walked up to the two friends. Mac Roth
sniffed the air and said, "I smell woman sweat."

"Damned old fool, you best keep your damned mouth
silent."

"But of course we will remain silent, your honor, for
we are lowly men that have never had the pleasure of one
so lovely and gentle," said Adian.

"You little shit, if I did not feel so bad I would kick
your rabbit ass from here to Emain Macha." Just then,
the horns from the fort began to sing their wailing song to
the countryside.

A single Alban warrior rode out of the gate with a red
cloth on the end of his stabbing spear. The red cloth
meant that he was a messenger and should not be
harmed. The six leaders mounted their horses and
headed to the road that led from the fort. As the warrior
approached, his spear was driven into the ground so there
could be no mistake about his real purpose. He then came
to the face of The Hound and spoke, "I come with a chal-

lenge of man to man combat between our champion Eagon mac Usheen of the darkland, subject of the most powerful king in the isles of the sky, the mighty Furbaide fer Benn. This warrior has been leader of the armies of Alba for more than twenty years. His feats of courage and valor are known as far as the great land of the long forest and they who suffered in defeat at the hands of Eagon. You will not be thought of as a coward if you refuse to battle, for only a fool would arm himself against such a mighty killer of the bravest of men. To do battle with the mighty Eagon is certain death."

Cuchulainn had heard many challenges in his short life, but this had been the most impressive. He thought for a minute and then began his response, "Bring forth the mighty Alban warrior. It will be good to battle with a combatant who has the courage to face The Hound of Ulster, for surely he knows the tales told of the thousands that are now in ash urns from Munster to the highland mountains of Alba. I salute him for facing certain death with such a challenge."

The Alban warrior spoke once again, "It will be necessary for you to send a hostage to guarantee no treachery fall upon our warrior and his charioteer."

Cuchulainn turned to his comrades, "I do not trust these dark ones. What do you say to this part of the challenge?"

Celtcha raised his voice,"You are right, these flesh-eaters are not ones to honor the ancient ways."

"I will go as the hostage," said Mac Roth, "for I will be no great loss if they kill me. And also, with my hearing, maybe I could overhear what plans they have in store for us."

It was agreed that Mac Roth had talents that could help if the siege lasted for a long period. So he returned to do his stay with the Albans. He felt a strange cold wind as he entered the fort and he felt the nostrils of some sort of animal touch his arm when he entered the hut of the king. "What sort of hostage is this? They send a worn out warrior with no eyes. Is this a joke by The Hound," shouted the king.

"Your majesty, I am the right hand of Cuchulainn. He looks to me for my experience and my special skills. You might say I am the right hand of The Hound."

"Well then, indeed we have an honored guest. Let us serve him from our fresh roasted meat."

As Mac Roth was handed his bowl, he sniffed, and smelled a sweet odor that was not that of beef or pork. He then took a small bite, shook his head and spoke, "My compliments to your cook."

This night Cuchulainn went among the camp women and took his choice among young and old. He had a fine cow and hog slaughtered for his meal. His cup would never be empty on this eve. His armor was brought out and Adian began to shine and polish all the metal surfaces. Gwydion came to him with a gift of a new dagger. Its tip was golden and the edges were as sharp as the tooth of a mountain bear. The grip had rubies and gold inlay on the top was a small release that opened a vial of poison that let the lethal liquid run the length of the blade. His warriors gave The Hound a small bag of golden bracelets and earrings. Bridget and Morrigan rubbed special oils onto his muscular body. These were blessed by the gods and would give him special healing abilities. The goddess Danu watched with interest and a little jealousy as the girls stroked the massive body of man-god. She had been watching the result of the human actions that were taking place in hopes of seeing what help the other gods were giving to the Albans.

Sunlight broke over the edge of the planet and ran like a river over the camp. The nightwatch began to awaken the entire camp, for on this day, no one would oversleep. The excitement could be felt as if electric waves were running the camp, except in the tent of The Hound. He slept, surrounded by the most beautiful women in the camp. Some were young and some were old, some were married and some were virgins. It did not matter, it was a traditional honor to sleep with a warrior before single combat.

It was time. The Hound came from his tent and dressed himself in his finest attire. His bold bronze helmet had just been molded and shined like gold, it came to a point on which perched a raven in honor of Danu. All his spears had been cleaned and blessed by the druid priest. His sword was sharpened and to the finest edge and his ax could shave the hair from one's head. The girls of the camp had woven the plaid wool strips of the tribe into braids of his hair and beard as he slept. Glistening skin and shining armor set off the long blond hair filled with color—a sight to see.

Adian had been up most of the night brushing the horses' manes and polishing the pieces of metal that adorn the chariot. He too had put on his finest attire. When Gwydion and Celtcha saw him in his best rags, they called him into Gwydion's tent. "You look fine Adian, but please allow us to put you in some gifts we have taken while on raids," said Celtcha. "But first we need to clean you up a little," cried Gwydion as she poured a bucket of water over his head. The makeover began.

Meanwhile, in the fort of Furbaide, the mood was not as excited. Eagon had been dressed for hours. He was long at prayer to all the gods who would listen. He prayed for his son who was in the world of past warriors and he prayed for the safety of his other son who would man his chariot. As he was readying himself for an honorable task, the king and Keiran were plotting for not so honorable actions. A plan for a mass attack during the one-on-one battle, was being laid out to some other officers who would be led by Kieran.

Cuchulainn stood in site of all the mass troops of Ulster men and women. He raised his sword and ax into the air and with a roar of a lion, he called out the warcry of the Ulster troops,"*Sliab Fuait!*" The warriors responded with the cry, over and over. Their hearts were filled with pride and they longed for battle. Anyone who would expect to catch these men and women warriors not ready for battle were going to be very much surprised.

The Hound heard the sound of horses' hooves pounding the earth and the roar made by a Celtic chariot. The sun was to his front and he had trouble seeing who was driving toward him. At first he thought that Eagon was making a surprise attack, but then he saw his faithful mounts snorting the morning dew from their nostrils and digging huge amounts of dirt from the Alban turf.

But who was that at the reins? As the chariot drew closer he saw a warrior with a golden shield on his back and a bronze breastplate. He wore a helmet that boasted a bull's head on top and plaid woolen pants. His boots were of deerskin and he even wore shin plates. As he came, he took the reins in one hand and pulled a gleaming sword from his side and yelled, "*Sliab Fuait.*" Much to the surprise of The Hound, it was Adian. His red hair was in warrior braids and he had the look of a great charioteer.

Pulling hard on the reins, Adian drew the steeds to a sliding halt and dismounted. "Now, who do we have here?" said The Hound.

106

"I am the one who has come to drive you to victory," boasted the young pup.

"If you drive as good as you look, we will have Eagon on his back in a short time."

Cuchulainn could hear the horns and yells for victory coming from the fort; this could only mean that Eagon was on his way. The Hound checked to see if all the throwing spears were in place and also his great shafted stabbing spear. He placed his ax on his hip and mounted behind Adian. When he took the flag of Ulster and raised it to its place on the chariot, the sound of five thousand men and women warriors could be heard in Emain Macha. As the surrounding hills came alive with the warcry and supporting yells for The Hound, the gates to the fort opened as an impressive Eagon moved forward to the fray.

The warriors of Alban began to follow their hero out to the place of battle. It was not unusual for the chiefs and officers to come to the battlefield, but on this day archers, missile throwers, and foot soldiers followed them. It was obvious that the cavalry had not come to the field, somewhat unusual since all other elements were there.

As Cuchulainn moved forward, Gavyn grabbed his arm, "Take this with you, for something is not right about this battle," said the youth. He then handed Adian a long bow and a quiver of arrows. "Do not let harm come to The Hound if there is a sign of treachery. Use this to buy time until we can come to your aid."

"Alright," said Adian.

Battle lines were drawn. There was a small creek that ran down the middle of a valley that formed a natural stadium. Both supporters were formed up to the high points on each side. As normal, both armies were in ranks and ready for action if need be. The hillside of the Ulster men was much more impressive due to a number advantage. The Albans were short due to the mass kill that had taken place only a few days before. Also they were known to have a cavalry that was thought to number around two thousand. This numbers game had giving the Ulster men a little too much confidence and they began to taunt their foes by showing their asses and genitals. Some stripped naked and repeatedly ran out to the battle line and screamed of their past victories and their bravery. Both sides did this, but no-one could start anything for fear of taking the honor from the two that were to fight one to one.

As the two warriors came out onto the field of combat, Cuchulainn saw for the first time the size of Eagon and his son. The Hound had trained for battle in the northern part of Alban, and had heard the stories told of the ancient giant warriors that had settled the south of the island before the great separation from the land of the great forest. It was said that they had come from far over the mountains to the east. At one time, they were covered with red hair all over their bodies and stood seven feet tall. Eagon was a close clone to the ancient ones and stood close to the seven-foot marker. His son was born of a mother from a small area between Leinster and Munster called Sid ar Femen. Eagon had taken her in a raid and decided to have children with her. The boys had her blue-grey eyes and their father's size. Noishu stood about six-foot-six and weighed over two hundred and twenty pounds. Eagon weighed close to three hundred pounds and had very little fat.

Despite the disadvantage of size, the two Ulster heroes were much quicker on their feet and of course Cuchulainn had the gifts of the special training. Adian looked like a tick on a hog as the four of them came close. "Damn, Cuchulainn, I seem too small to be of any help."

"You do not need to be big to drive a chariot or throw a spear," said The Hound in hopes of encouraging the youth.

The two chariots came to a stop about ten feet from each other. "Turn and go home Cuchulainn and we can all avoid more dying."

"This is not between me and you, Eagon. I suggest that you send out the King who took the long vision from our land," answered The Hound. "Well, I guess that you will not go home, and I am bound by honor to defeat you. Let's get this over with."

The chariots turned away and went some twenty-five yards on either side of the creek. The chariot drivers assumed a position behind the front shield and then removed their shields to place them at the front to give extra protection from the spears and arrows. The horses of both chariots sprung forward in a blind charge at their fellow equines. The Hound drew a throwing spear and at about ten yards sent one toward the lead horse. Noishu was well-experienced at driving a chariot in battle which was more difficult than this one-on-one fighting. He pulled hard with his right lead and quickly changed directions. The spear drove into the side of the chariot, barely missing the leg of Noishu. As they passed by the chariot of The Hound, Eagon let a large rock fly at their lead horse. It smashed onto the horse's back hip and the squeal of pain could be heard by both troops. A cheer went up from the Albans.

The horse began to limp and this slowed down the control of the chariot. Adian pulled away and stopped. "What are you doing?" cried The Hound.

Adian jumped out and ran to the front of the horse

and said, *"qureim con divatt koch pondoctor que kiena."* He then returned to his place. He snapped the reins and both horses bolted back into battle. Cuchulainn did not have time to ask what had happened as he turned sideways to avoid a throwing spear. Adian spun the chariot around and to the surprise of every one involved, he was behind the chariot of Eagon. This exposed the back of the two warriors. Cuchulainn quickly grabbed a spear with each hand and let them fly. The missiles were thrown with skill and power and one went deep into the left thigh of Noishu who bellowed in pain. The second was headed straight for the back Eagon, but he had placed his shield over his back for just such situations. The spear glanced off the shield as Eagon took the reins from his son.

Noishu slid the spear out, but it did not come easily since it lodged in the bone. He ripped a piece of plaid from his cloak and tied it around his thigh. This helped the bleeding, but blood was running all over the floor of the chariot and this made it difficult for Eagon to plant his feet to throw a spear accurately. Cuchulainn saw what was going on and knew Eagon was at a disadvantage. An experienced driver would have swung around and circled the other chariot until a kill was made, but Adian was not experienced. He smelled victory and went in for the kill—big mistake.

When Eagon saw that the chariot was coming close, he pulled out his stabbing spear and rolled from his chariot and fell in front of the oncoming chariot. Just as The Hound cried out, "Turn!" Eagon planted the wide blade and the stout shaft in the ground in front of the charging horses. Horrible sounds came from the lead horse as the blade ripped into its chest. Eagon rolled to the side and watched as the chariot flipped into the air sending both warriors into the sky. Another cheer went up as it looked like this would be the day of Eagon.

Adian was in a dream state as he lay on the ground wondering what had just happened. He looked good on the ground in his new clothes, although they had become somewhat dirty. He started to dust his new garments, but the timing was not good for Eagon was charging at him with his ax. No place to run . . . no place to hide. It looked to be the end of a much too short life, but what will be, will be. He closed his eyes as the giant warrior took a circular swing and the blade was on a downward path. Eyes closed, he waited for death. Damn, he was just ten years old and had known only a lonely old whore that was at the end of her career. He wanted to sail in a boat and he wanted to drink wine instead of ale just one time. But now it was all over.

He heard a thud as the ax blade hit the ground next to him. He had not seen the flying figure of Cuchulainn smash into the body on Eagon. They rolled over and over pulling and tearing at anything they could get a hold on. The Hound had a finger in a large nostril and Eagon was trying to give a good kick in the balls, *caber fae,* to Cuchulainn. Eagon put his arms around the chest of The Hound and squeezed with great strength. The air rushed out of The Hound's lungs and the rush shot toward the Alban troops. Some were blown to the ground, others had their kilts blown above their heads.

They rolled toward the creek. The Hound was in big trouble and he knew it. He was turning blue in the face so he decided it was time for a warp spasm. As he started to make the transformation, they rolled into the creek and the cold water stopped his spasm. He was now in a heap of shit and he had to try one more move. He gathered all his strength and called for the salmon leap. He shot from the arms of Eagon, leaving a little piece of ear in the giant's mouth. The Hound landed on the dry ground and drew his sword. The giant was without a weapon.

Cuchulainn thought that maybe it was the honorable thing to allow such a great warrior to have one more chance, then he came to his senses and drove his sword through the stomach of Eagon. The giant called to The Hound to come closer as he was dying. Cuchulainn did not want to give this one a second shot at him so he kept his distance. Eagon gasped, "Take my son into your ranks, for he has no love for Furbaide or the animal-man-son."

"Animal-man-son, what the hell is that?"

"You will find out soon enough," and then the last breath left his body.

Adian had gone to do battle with Noishu and found a wounded wolf to be somewhat of a problem. As a matter of fact Noishu was chasing Adian around the chariot. "Stop," called The Hound. "Your father wanted you to join us in our battle with Furbaide."

"It will give me great pleasure to kill the king and especially the animal he calls a son."

As the five thousand Ulster men cheered at the results of the battle, the plan of Kieran started to take action. As the regular troops began to move forward, the three warriors found that they were behind the battle lines of the Albans. Cuchulainn turned to Adian and said, "Get the horses that can run and bring them here." Just as this took place, Cuchulainn heard the sound of battle horns coming from the fortress. The gates opened and out rode the king, Kieran, and his daughter warriors. They were on a path straight for Cuchulainn and Noishu. Adian had done his work well and they were all on horseback in a few minutes. Adian looked back at the horsemen coming their way. One of the daughters had something on the end of her spear. "Come on boy," barked Cuchulainn.

"Wait Hound, there is something I must see closer." Adian then saw the head of his friend Mac Roth on the spear of Furbaide's older daughter.

"Damn it fool, come quickly, there is nothing we can do for him now," called The Hound.

"Oh yes there is." Adian reached for the long bow and drew the string tight. The arrow took flight and planted itself in the eye of the young princess. She screamed out in pain. Adian said quietly, "goodbye my old friend."

The three rode to the Ulster battle line and Cuchulainn gave the command to attack. The warriors were ready for a fight and all weapons were at the ready. The missile-throwers launched their missiles, axes, swords, spears, sharp poles with metal points, rocks of all sizes, large mallets, farm implements, and anything that met the occasion. They ran headlong into the ranks of the Alban warriors and the killing began.

Furbaide held back his cavalry, still waiting for a sign from Cernunnos as to what he would do to keep his promise of help. The king had just lost a daughter to the battle, but he was not a man of soft feelings and her loss would pass. His major concern was to win this battle. He still had his secret weapon that he was holding back, Kieran.

Cernunnos was about to play his card in this game and it was a good one. The other gods would have to be very creative to outdo him this day.

In the field of death from the battle two days ago, there came a strange red glow from the decaying bodies. The buzzards and ravens that were enjoying their feast began to fly away. There was a movement in the field. It was located behind the battle lines of the Ulster men. The field crawled with movement and warriors began to rise and take up what weapons they could find. Those without weapons pulled branches from trees and gathered as a troop. This was a sight that no-one would have hoped to witness. The stench began to drift to the hilltop where they would once more join in the battle.

Cuchulainn was watching the battle with his leaders from behind the battle line, about half way up the hill. The battle was going heavily in the favor of the Ulster men. From behind where the camp followers had been watching the fight, there came terrifying screams. The leaders turned to see the first wave of dead warriors come over the peak of the hill. A camp follower ran at one and ran a spear through him and in return, the walking dead grabbed him and ripped his throat out with his teeth.

Panic fell on the leaders. Cuchulainn spoke first, "What the hell will we do now?"

"I know how to kill the living, but killing the dead . . . that's another story all together."

Gwydion turned to Gavyn, "You always have an answer for everything. Why don't you come up with something for this?"

"Give me a little time to think this out, you know this is not something you see everyday."

Furbaide looked to the hill, "Ha, ha, what a way to help, this is wonderful. Me leading an army of the dead. I will be talked about throughout history, and now I may become master of the world, with an animal-son and an army of the dead. Attack, attack!"

There were two more sets of eyes watching the battlesite. The goddess Danu, spoke with her friend Rosmerta, "Well what can you do to top this?" asked Rosmerta.

"I don't know, this is pretty good."

"I will think of something for Gavyn to present. He is a good prospect for king of Ulster and this could get The Hound on his side."

"I have another question, are you hoping to get another roll with The Hound?"

"You bet I am, he was the best I have had in my three thousand years."

"Well, then count me in for the next time or I will not help you."

"Sure, he's just a man."

Things were not good for the Ulster heroes. The army was now trapped between the dead and living troops of the Albans. Furbaide made a strong flanking move and cut the Ulster men into two forces. They could not retreat due to the walking dead and it was time for the leaders to make some move.

"Alright, alright, let's get organized here. I will make the person who comes up with a way to kill the dead the next king of Ulster."

"Does that include me?" asked Gwydion.

"Of course it includes you."

"I just had an idea," yelled Gavyn.

"He's always got an idea and it usually includes my daughter," mocked Gwydion.

"Cuchulainn, didn't you kill a thousand troops and another thousand chieftains and kings with blades attached to your chariot?" asked Gavyn.

"Yes, but they were alive."

"Well, consider that if you chop them up real fine they can't kill our warriors."

"It will work. Adian get the blades on the chariot."

Adian and two warriors went fast to work putting the

blades on in record time. "Come Adian, let's go kill some dead people."

"Cuchulainn, I have never driven the chariot with the blades on, I will get you and me killed."

"Damn, that's right. So much for that idea."

A voice came from behind the leaders. "I can drive a chariot with blades." They all turned to see Noishu, bandaged leg, but ready for battle. "I know it seems strange, but I loved my twin brother and I am sure that the beast-son ate him."

"Are you in condition to drive and fight?" asked The Hound.

"I will drive like the wind and you will kill 'till you tire of doing so."

The two warriors mounted the platform of the chariot and burst toward the top of the hill. When they neared the ridge, they were amazed at the devastation that the cadaver troops had carried onto the battlefield. Most of the camp followers lay dead or dying. The troops that were sent to protect the Ulster's rear were fighting bravely but they could take no advantage. Killing the dead was not an easy thing to do. The Ulster men were falling like flies. Seeing the faces of the mindless dead, Cuchulainn urged Noishu to drive the horses straight into their ranks. The Hound was armed with his huge ax and began the harvest of the dead. The blades were working to perfection as body parts flew into the air. The horses were knocking the dead warriors down and the blades mulched them. Cuchulainn kept the attackers off the chariot as well as helping to dismember arms and other parts. Seeing the success The Hound was having, the other leaders mounted blades to their chariots and rode into the graveyard battle. The warriors that were defending the rear could now turn on the Alban cavalry and put them in a vice.

Furbaide looked to the hill and saw his deadly troops being turned into chips of flesh. He looked up and saw a thousand foot soldiers running into battle against his horsemen. He sensed the end, so now it was time to send his new warrior to the front. He turned to Kieran and cried, "Charge!" Excited by the smell of blood, the animal-son advanced toward the leaders of the Ulster men. He had with him the special troop of killer warriors who had been specially picked for their heartless methods of killing and their lack of compassion.

Furbaide called to his remaining daughter to follow him back to the fortress. He was prepared for these circumstances and had an escape route laid out. Kieran turned to see the king and his sister going through the gate. He was committed to his attack and caught the friends of The Hound off guard. He and his trained killers cut their way easily through the ranks that protected the leaders. Gavyn, Gwydion and Celtcha had joined Cuchulainn in the harvest of the dead and left Adian, Bridget and Morrigan to support the battle taking place down below.

To the young one's surprise, Kieran's forces broke through and were upon them. They all three stood back to back fighting as hard as they could. Kieran watched Morrigan cut down two of his best warriors. She was a sight to his animal instinct and he knew that he must have this woman.

While running her chariot through the living corpses, Gwydion saw the bad situation that befell her daughters. Her job finished, she turned her horses on a path to save her children. As she drew closer, she saw Kieran charge Morrigan and knock her sword from her

hand. Gwydion's hard heart fell to her feet, for surely this was the end for the young warrior princess. She loosened the reins so the horses would go faster. Her spear was in hand and she let fly at the animal-man. Her aim was good, but just as she threw, the animal bent over and the spear shot over his head. Much to her surprise she watched the hairy arm wrap around the petite waist of Morrigan. He lifted her onto his horse and rode away, his private guard falling away behind him.

Gwydion pulled up, dismounted, and smashed the skulls of two Albans that were attacking Bridget. Adian had fought well enough that all that were upon him retreated. "Are you alright?" said Gwydion.

"Yes mother, I'll be okay." It was then that the mother saw that Bridget had been stabbed in the side. Gwydion had hoped to pursue Kieran and Morrigan, but she was now forced to help her other daughter stop the bleeding. She looked to the fortress gate in time to see the animal ride in with Morrigan still in his grasp.

The men of Ulster had won the day. Cheers could be heard from all over the battlefield."*Sliab Fuait*" was repeated over and over. Cuchulainn returned to the side of his friends and warriors. They were all ready to advance and take the fortress with no effort. Now was payday for the whores and the slave dealers would fill their chains with good samples of manhood and womanhood. The next phase was to let the troops proceed with the pillaging and The Hound must recover the long vision for Ulster.

Only one was not happy, as she wrapped the side of her child. Gwydion's loss was more painful than she could have ever had imagined. As the ale horns were being filled, Cuchulainn looked to Gwydion, "Here, you need to have this, it will help," said The Hound as he handed her a horn of ale.

119

"I will never be happy until I get my daughter back from that man animal."

"Don't worry, we will be with you," said The Hound with much sympathy.

There was much activity going on in the fortress when Kieran came through the door pulling Morrigan behind him. The king, queen, and the one daughter were ready to load into the wagons outside the rear entrance of the fort. The king seemed a little surprised to see Kieran. "Well good, I see that you have survived your first battle."

"Indeed I have, no thanks to you," growled the animal man.

"What did you expect me to do, stand there and protect you from the big, bad Ulster men?"

"I needed no protection, only support."

"You had support from the best warriors I could muster for you."

"They fought well and my back was covered. But you—you turned and ran. . . . after all these months of you telling of your mighty victories. It is apparent that all your victories belonged to Eagon."

Squirming, the king tried to change the subject, "I see you have captured a woman, that's a great sign of boldness in battle."

"She killed two of your hand-picked warriors."

"All this is quite good, but we must go now. Just sacrifice her to Cernunnos and we will all be on our way to the land of the great forest."

"No," Kieiran growled.

"What did you say to me? NO?"

"That's right, no harm will come to her, she is mine."

"Well, well, what do we have here?" smirked the king. "It would seem that the animal man has human feelings and we cannot have that, now can we?"

At this, the king drew his dagger and lunged toward Morrigan. His feet never touched the floor. Kieran lifted the king up to his massive face and said, "You have taught me well, my father, feelings are for the weak. I will prove to you that I am not weak." The claw-like fingernails penetrated the breastplate that had stopped so many attempts on the king's life. With one pull, it flew across the room. The claws then entered the chest and pulled a still-beating heart from the cavity. The king's face had a look of disbelief that made Keiran laugh out loud. He then ate the heart in two bites. "Thanks, father, for the gift of the long vision. Since I was cheated from gaining the gifts from Cuchulainn, it is proper that I retain your inheritance." As he finished the last bite, he turned to face his mother and sister's attack. He picked them both up by the back of the necks and smashed their faces together. The force was so great that no one could recognize who these people were.

Kieran yelled to his guards, "The wagons are full with all that we need, let us go to the land of the Great Forest." As he was leaving, pulling Morrigan behind him, he turned to the dying parents and sibling and said, "Thanks for the hospitality, you were a great family."

The Ulster men were busy chasing down the defeated Albans. Their plight was to be sold into slavery and the gold collected was given to the till to pay for the campaign. The fortress was being stripped of all things of value and the normal rape and pillage was taking place. Those who did not escape or were wounded would suffer the other alternative. They were held for sacrifice at the winter solstice.

Cuchulainn and his mates went straight to the hut of the king. What they saw was not what they expected. There was only a dead king, queen, and princess. It was obvious by the mutilations that Kieran was far more brutal than any warrior they had yet faced. The long vision had once again been stolen and would not return to Ulster.

"I have not accomplished my quest," shouted The Hound, "I must hunt down this flesh-eating man beast and bring back his blood to our new king Gavyn." Gavyn stood shocked. He had heard The Hound say it, but this was the first time that he had time to think about it. "You will lead our forces back across the icebridge as soon as possible. You will assume the position of king and rule fairly over Ulster."

"My thanks to The Hound, I will do my best to be a fair king. I will need a queen. Gwydion, may I take Bridget as my queen?"

"I will go with The Hound in search of Morrigan. It would be good if I knew Bridget was in safe hands. Yes . . . if it is her wish as well."

Over the next few days the Ulster mens' baggage train was ready to go. All that had any value had been loaded onto the wagons and it was time to go home and enjoy the victory. There was a mass burning of the fallen comrades. The druids prayed for them to enjoy the land of those killed in battle. Gavyn and Bridget were married, but that's another story. Celtcha decided to serve the young king as his adviser and return to his love—Mother Ulster.

The train pulled out onto the trail home. Three figures sat atop a hill and watched them disappear. Cuchulainn, Gwydion and Adian were saddened by the loss of the blind one who kept their spirits high. They could not be sad for long, their chase was about to begin. They mounted their horses and started west. They heard a voice call out to them, they turned and saw a lone horse-

man coming up fast. It was Noishu. He stopped beside The Hound and ask, "Do you have room for one more?"

"Why would you wish to join us when there is only danger in our paths?"

"I am used to danger and there is nothing left for me here, besides someone needs to teach this young charioteer to run with blades."

"You are welcome to go with us into the unknown," smiled The Hound.